FIGHT FOR ME

WRATH JAMES WHITE

Fight For Me
By Wrath James White
Copyright © 2020 by Wrath James White
All rights reserved.

Without limiting the rights under copyright reserved above, no part of this publication may be reproduced, stored, or introduced into a retrieval system, or transmitted in any form, or by any means (electronic, mechanical, photocopying or otherwise) without the prior written permission of the copyright owner, except in the case of brief quotations embodied within critical articles and reviews or works within the public domain.

This book is a work of fiction. People, places, events, and situations are the product of the author's imagination. Any resemblance to actual persons, living or dead, or historical events, is coincidental.

1

I ALMOST LAUGHED WHEN I LANDED THAT FIRST KICK TO HIS inner thigh. The loud "Thwack!" of my shin bone cutting deep into his leg echoed throughout the gym. His thick quadricep muscle reddened immediately. The surprised look on his face was priceless. It told me he hadn't properly prepared for this fight. He had taken me lightly because I was a woman.

He was a boxer. That meant he wasn't used to being kicked. Most people underestimate how painful a kick to the thigh, particularly the inner thigh or the hamstrings, can be. My shins were conditioned from long hours kicking the bottom of the heavy bag, one thousand kicks a day. The bag in my gym held one hundred and fifty pounds of sand and strips of leather packed down and compressed so that the bottom felt just like concrete, and so did my shins after eleven months of that punishment. But now, both of my shins were denser than baseball bats, and I swung them at his thigh with full power, digging my sharp bone into his soft tissue like I was swinging for a home run.

I saw him stifle a grunt. Fighters didn't make noises

when they got hit. They didn't wince or show any indication of pain. It was considered a pussy move. You were never supposed to show weakness, let your opponent know that anything they did had any effect on you. It gave your opponent confidence, and made him (or her) braver and more aggressive. You were supposed to take it and keep your expression as stoic as possible, until you were ready to quit. And that's what he did – or tried to do. His expression hardened as he suppressed the pain, but I saw it. I had hurt him.

He threw a straight right, putting his full force behind it. He didn't care that I was a woman. I had hurt him, and he wanted some payback. More than that, he wanted the prize. He wanted me. But I saw the punch coming and easily slipped it. His fist sailed harmlessly over my left shoulder, and I landed another leg kick, this time to the top of his thigh, coming down with the full force of my weight, and I am not a small woman.

Nearly six foot, one hundred and eighty pounds of muscle and curves. In my running group, they call women like me "Athenas", and we have our own race category. I always found that amusing, because it was also my name. In mixed martial arts, I was a heavyweight. If I was a man, I'd have to be more than twenty pounds heavier to fight as a heavyweight. But women are supposed to be smaller, more dainty. A man has to be over two hundred and five pounds to be a heavyweight. A woman? One hundred and eighty pounds. It was an odd bias. I mean, this guy was over two hundred and twenty pounds, and I was kicking his ass.

I followed the leg kick with a kick to his ribs that doubled him over. There was no hiding this pain as the air whooshed out of his lungs and he bent over, tucking his arm against his side to protect it against further damage, but refusing to go down. He had heart. Most fighters did. You had to have more courage than your average guy just to set foot inside the ring or the cage. But getting punched in the body is nothing like getting a shin slammed into your ribcage. A shin kick is like a baseball bat swung with full force. Not many people could take that, and I could see the shock of it in his eyes. This guy, for all his size and muscle, wasn't in my league. He was wasting my time. I decided to end it quickly.

He recovered from the body kick enough to throw a desperate left hook that I easily blocked. I slipped a right cross, then threw a flying knee that caught him under the chin and dropped him to the mat. I didn't normally use flashy moves like that. I was showboating, putting an exclamation point on the beat down I was administering this loser. He was still conscious, but just barely. His pupils were wide and unfocused, and his body went stiff like those old black and white movies of The Mummy, arms and legs outstretched and flailing. I mounted him and began to rain down punches and elbows, bruising and bloodying his once handsome face. His nose split down the center from his forehead to his left nostril and smashed against his left cheek. His right eye swelled and shut. He was a beautiful man. Was. Blond hair, bluish-gray eyes, tall, just an inch or two over six feet, with a chiseled physique and a boyish smile that was both charming and devilish. He had matinee idol looks. And I had a moment of regret that he hadn't been the one. But I wasn't looking for a pretty boy. I was looking for a man. A man strong enough that I could submit to him, call him my Master and become his slave. And this bleeding piece of meat beneath me wasn't it. Perhaps I could keep him as my slave. I considered straddling his ruined face and forcing him to get me off with his tongue under threat of further punishment. The only thing that stopped me was the certainty that he'd enjoy it. Besides, I still had my ex-husband for that. Out of frustration, and perhaps a bit of pure stubborn meanness, I put him in an arm bar. I didn't wait for him to tap before I arched my back, straightened my legs, and snapped his arm at the elbow. I could hear the ligaments tear and pop with a moist ripping sound.

"OW! Fuck! My fucking arm! You broke my fucking arm!"

That stuff about not showing any pain to your opponent no longer applied once you were beaten.

"It'll heal," I said. "Now get your weak ass out of my gym, pretty boy."

I know it was harsh, but I had warned him when he signed up. I warned them all. Come in here unprepared and you will get hurt. But men will take just about any risk for the promise of pussy. And what I was offering was all the pussy a man could want, any time, any way he wanted it. All he had to do was fight for me ... and win.

2

MY NAME IS ATHENA TOSCANO, AND I LIKE TO FIGHT.

It began right after my divorce. My husband, Steve, had been a child. Good looking, well-built, but helpless and weak. He spent hours in the gym making sure his body remained a masterpiece of physical beauty. But it was useless muscle. I had no illusions about him ever protecting me. His muscles were his one and only deterrent. If the sight of him didn't frighten off a potential assailant, he would be all out of tricks. He had never been in a fight in his life and avoided confrontation as if the slightest argument would result in mutually assured destruction. The result was that he did whatever I asked him to. It was like having my very own submissive. In fact, I'm pretty sure he would have let me chain him up and whip him if I had asked. But I didn't want a submissive man. Not as a husband. I wanted someone powerful and dominant. Not an equal. A superior.

When I first walked into the kickboxing gym, I wasn't looking for a man. I was just trying to lose some weight and get in shape. I had just left my ex for good and needed to drop a few pounds and tone up before putting myself back on the market. And I had no intention of waiting. I didn't need a cooling off period, time to find myself or to mourn the dissolution of my marriage. Steve had been a mistake, one I'd had plenty of time to reflect on. He was a nice guy, a good-looking guy, the kind you were supposed to marry, the kind any other woman would have been happy to have, but I needed more than that.

Steve's inability to keep a job should have been the first indication of his worthlessness as a man. He would quit a job for any reason. One job made his back hurt. The other was too early for him to wake up. Another was too late and interfered with his workout schedule. Not challenging enough. Too challenging. Didn't pay enough. The boss was an asshole. His co-workers were assholes. And on. And on. Steve had rich parents who would pay all of his bills for him. So, a proper work ethic had never been instilled in him. He'd never needed to work. If he had bills to pay, he could just call mama. Needed a new car because he got drunk and wrecked the old one? Call mama. Money for the deposit on a new apartment? Mama. I suspected early on that he only took jobs because he knew I wanted him to. Because he knew I couldn't respect a man who lived off his mama and couldn't make a living on his own. In the end, I lost respect for him anyway. That's when I knew I had to leave.

We didn't fight. We didn't argue. I just told him it wasn't working and that I wanted a divorce. He seemed relieved, as if he had wanted out too, but just hadn't had the balls to ask for a divorce. And that was probably the truth of it. Our marriage had rested upon his cowardice.

So, a week after my divorce, I walked into The Monster Maker Muay Thai Kickboxing and MMA Academy and signed up for one year of lessons. I didn't want to do one of those stupid cardio-kickboxing classes where overweight housewives flailed impotently at pads using horrible form and non-existent technique. My dad had been a boxer. I grew up watching boxing. I knew bad form when I saw it, and I cringed at the thought of looking like any of those ridiculous people. I wanted someone who would teach me for real and correct me when I made a mistake. So, I joined a real gym.

Monster Maker trained real fighters. Professionals and amateurs. I would be sparring with a guy one day and watching him fight on TV the next. It was exciting. I felt like I was part of something. But that feeling of belonging wasn't the only thing I felt. Watching men with bodies like Greek gods beat the hell out of each other was more than a little arousing. The first time I sat in on the MMA class and watched one of the amateur fighters get triangle choked by one of the pros, I could feel the wetness spread between my thighs. I was so wet I had to look down at my shorts to make sure I wasn't dripping right through them. That's when I began taking MMA as well as Muay Thai.

I did everything the fighters did. When they ran, I ran. When they hit the weight room, I was right behind them. I did all the drills and calisthenics they did. I did the heavy bag work, worked the focus mitts, and even began sparring. I was hooked. It was no longer just about getting into shape. I loved the violence. I loved seeing men hurt each other, struggling for dominance over one another. I even liked it when they hurt me.

The first time I sparred, it was against a guy two inches shorter and twenty pounds lighter than me. I was almost insulted. I had been training for a couple months by this point, and my body had hardened with the type of muscle women usually tried to avoid gaining, my endurance was up, and my technique was improving. The feminist in me wanted to protest that I was ready take on a guy my size, but I remained silent out of respect for my trainers. I was still quietly fuming about it when I stepped out onto the mat and locked up with my opponent, confident I would easily overpower him. I remained confident right up until the little guy took me down with a hip toss, wrapped me up like a pretzel, and almost choked me unconscious. That was the first time I had an orgasm during training. It was shocking and unexpected. I was mortified.

One minute I was struggling, fighting to free myself from a rear-naked choke, feeling my opponent's strength and superior technique effortlessly overcoming my resistance. Then, as his forearm clamped down on the sides of my neck, compressing my carotid arteries and choking off the blood supply to my brain, I began getting lightheaded, and that's when the orgasm came ripping through me like an electric shock. He released his hold on me, and I collapsed onto the canvas, struggling to catch my breath.

"Are you okay?" the little wiry guy who'd just choked me out asked, worried that he had hurt me as I lay there on the mat, trembling.

"It-it's my fault. I should have tapped," I answered as I sat up, still uncertain of exactly what had happened, but the wet spot on my shorts had answered that question. Embarrassed, I ran into the dressing room and quickly showered and changed. When I left the women's locker room, intending to slip out without talking to anyone, and debating whether or not I would ever come back, the wiry guy was still there, rolling with another one of the new guys. When he saw me, he quickly tapped the new guy out, then ran over to me and caught me before I could make my escape out the front door.

"Hey, I hope you didn't get freaked out. The first time I got choked unconscious, I pissed and shit myself. It's a normal reaction. Nothing to be embarrassed about. It happens to everyone."

I realized he thought I had pissed myself when he choked me unconscious. I wasn't sure if that was better or worse than him knowing I'd had an orgasm.

"If you come early tomorrow, I'll show you a couple different ways to defend and escape that hold. My name's Dillon."

He held out his hand and I shook it, timidly.

"Athena."

"Oh, I know who you are. Everybody knows you in here. We were just talking about how you train like a beast. You put some of the fighters in here to shame. Are you planning to compete?"

"Oh, I don't know. I hadn't really thought about it. I figured I was too old."

"You're not old. What are you? Twenty-five?"

"Twenty-nine."

Dillon waved it off.

"We've got guys in here that didn't have their first fight until they were in their thirties. Besides, women's MMA is still in its infancy. The pool of competitors isn't that deep yet. You can get a title fight after less than ten fights. You should think about it."

I promised him I would consider it.

"And you'll come early tomorrow so we can work on a few things?"

"Y-yeah. Okay. Thanks," I said, before hurrying out the door. I was no longer embarrassed. No longer thinking about quitting. Now, I was thinking about fighting. And more than that, I was thinking about fucking Dillon.

3

THE NEXT DAY I COULD BARELY PAY ATTENTION AT WORK. I WAS like a zombie as I went about my job at the hair salon making rich people prettier. I listened to their stories of cheating husbands, boring husbands, fat husbands, workaholic husbands, impotent husbands, and the occasional confession of their own infidelity. I smiled and nodded and offered words of advice and vapid platitudes like "everything happens for a reason" and "the only constant is change."

My best friend, Becca, a loud, boisterous, butch lesbian who wore her hair in a bleached blonde pompadour, kept eying me all day. Today, like almost every day, Becca wore a plain, black, v-neck t-shirt without a bra. Her large grapefruit-sized breasts bobbled about freely beneath her shirt, her eternally erect nipples jabbing urgently at the cotton fabric. Her crisply starched and pressed Levi jeans were cuffed at the bottom, and her black combat boots were shined to a high gloss. To top it all off, she wore a pink flower in her hair. To be ironic, I was certain. She both celebrated and secretly loathed her own femininity.

It was Becca who had suggested I take up kickboxing.

She used to compete and had even held an amateur title once. Now, she mainly hung out in nightclubs drinking and picking up chicks. Her new ambition was to be a techno DJ, but for now, being a hair stylist paid much, much better.

"What's going on with you today? You've been grinning all afternoon like you're hiding a vibrator in your panties. What's up?" Becca asked.

She had a rather blunt way with words. She also knew me much too well. Becca was working on one of her oldest clients. The woman had been coming to Becca to get her hair washed, cut, and colored for nearly as long as Becca had been a stylist, following her from salon to salon. I sometimes wondered if the woman had a crush on Becca. The woman was married with three children, but I had been around enough to know that didn't mean a damn thing.

"If I tell you, you'll think I'm crazy."

"If you don't, I definitely will. You've been acting all spaced out and giddy all day. You in love or something?"

I could feel every ear in the salon perk up, waiting to hear what new development had taken place in my love life. I was used to it. Half the reason most of our clients came to the salon was to listen in on the gossip about our sex lives. Bored, frustrated housewives and high-powered professionals with no time for a social life, living vicariously through the wild young hairdressers they paid hundreds of dollars to do what they could have easily done for themselves at home. The more shocking and salacious our stories, the more frequently they came back. My divorce had almost doubled my weekly appointments. What housewife didn't want to hear about a woman who had managed to regain her freedom? My escape from my own nuptial malaise gave hope to all of them.

"Well, I was doing Jujitsu with this guy at the gym. We

Fight For Me 13

were kind of sparring. He was smaller than me, so I thought I could take him. I was a little pissed that my trainer paired me up with a guy twenty pounds lighter than me. You know, I've been training my ass off and it felt like he wasn't taking me seriously because I'm a woman. But this guy ... he just manhandled me. He almost choked me unconscious."

"What a dick! You get guys like that in the gym all the time. They feel threatened by a strong woman and want to put her in her place. Assholes!" Becca said.

But I shook my head. "No. No, it wasn't like that. It felt like he wasn't taking it easy on me because he respected me. He was just treating me like anyone else in the gym, like one of the guys. Anyway, he was choking me, and I couldn't get away, and I felt helpless. You know, really helpless. And I never feel helpless. I've always been the one in control. In all my relationships. Even during sex. I'm not some dainty little flower. I've been this height since seventh grade. I used to kick all the boys' asses when I was little. So, this feeling was something completely new."

Now Becca began to really listen. She leaned her client's head back into the sink almost absentmindedly, washing it and combing it on instinct, as she'd done a thousand times.

"And?" Becca asked.

"I think I had an orgasm."

"What?"

There was a collective gasp of shock. The woman I was working on, Marie Claire, also a long-time client who'd been coming to me for more than five years, let out a little chuckle.

"Oh, honey, that's normal," she said. "I love being choked during sex. It's the only way I can come during regular intercourse," Marie said. She was the owner of a local modeling agency and loved being scandalous despite the fact that she was three years past her sixtieth birthday.

"Marie! You're terrible."

She laughed. "It's true. A lot of women are into that. Don't you like being choked during sex?" Marie asked, addressing all the other women in the salon, who just stared at her blankly, some slowly shaking their heads.

"Oh, you're just a bunch of prudes. Anyway, darling, it's nothing to worry about."

Becca finally let out the laugh she was holding in.

"I don't know what's funnier, picturing you getting choked out, or picturing your face after you realized you just came during a sparring session. So, what? Are you into this little man now? I thought little guys weren't your type? You like big strong men," Becca said.

"Well, he is strong. He's just not very big. Anyway, I'm not sure I'm really into him."

"You just want him to choke you again?"

"Yes. I mean, no. I don't know. It wasn't really being choked that did it, it was being overpowered like that, I think. It was feeling so helpless, like he could have really hurt me if he wanted to. I felt out of control. It's like, that's what I've always wanted to feel when I'm with a man. But most men are really a bunch of pussies and mama's boys. It's hard to find a real man."

This time, everyone in the salon nodded in agreement.

I finished Marie's hair and made an appointment with her for next week. She was my last client of the day. I could feel Becca's eyes staring at me as I twisted my long red hair into one long braid and checked my makeup in the mirror.

"Be careful. Some men are pussies, but some men are dangerous assholes. You're a big, strong, bad ass bitch, but you're not a man."

"No. I'm better," I said. Because that's what I would have normally said. That's what I would have said just twenty-four hours ago, before I was nearly choked unconscious by a guy who looked like he should have been teaching history to sixth graders. When I say I'm not a small woman, I mean I can bench press a hundred and fifty pounds, squat two-fifty, and curl thirty-five pound dumbbells. Even before I started working out like a madwoman, I'd been too much for most men to handle; now, it was going to be twice as hard to find a man who could tame me. If I was lucky enough to have found one who might be up for the task, I wasn't going to let fear, or something as insignificant as a few inches in height, deter me.

Tame me? Is that really what I wanted? To be tamed and broken? A small, hidden part of myself, deep in my subconscious, answered back emphatically. *Yes.* I went in the back room to change into my workout clothes.

4

DILLON HAD TOLD ME TO BE THERE AT 3 P.M. REGULAR classes didn't start until six. Most days I got there at five so I could warm up and do my one thousand kicks on the heavy bag before class began. Some of the pro-fighters arrived as early as four. I tried to get there at four to work out with the pros as often as possible, whenever I didn't have a client scheduled. Today, I had rescheduled my later clients. That meant a longer day tomorrow, but it would also mean a full hour alone with Dillon.

The Monster Maker Muay Thai Kickboxing and MMA Academy was a seven thousand square foot warehouse. A big, gray building in an industrial area neighboring a cabinet warehouse, an auto shop that specialized in rebuilding old antique cars, and a plumbing and air-conditioning company. The cartoonish metal sign above the door was the only thing remotely aesthetically appealing about the place. From the outside, it looked no different than the other warehouses.

The inside was slightly better. It had a large sixteen-foot boxing ring, a twenty-foot cage, five hundred square feet of wrestling mats, a weight room, cardio area, and locker rooms with showers. A dozen muay thai heavy bags hung along the back wall along with three speed bags, two double-end bags, and a teardrop-shaped bag for practicing knees and uppercuts. Mirrors dominated the wall opposite the mats, so you could watch yourself while you shadow-boxed. The walls were painted dark purple, almost black, with deep wine red borders.

When I walked in, Dillon was already on the mat, working techniques on an MMA practice dummy.

"Hey, Athena! Glad you could make it. I was just working on an anaconda choke. Drop your stuff off in the locker room and I'll show you."

I smiled.

"Okay. Be right back."

Normally we take some time to stretch and warm up, but the minute I stepped out onto the mat, Dillon was already demonstrating moves on me, showing me different escapes from various choke holds, the triangle choke, the rear-naked, the guillotine, side chokes, and finally, the anaconda.

"I didn't know you were this good. How come you don't compete?"

"I do, every now and then. I'm just too busy at work to do this full-time. I have a little start-up company I'm trying to get off the ground."

I nodded and didn't ask any more questions. It seemed like everyone I knew had a start-up company. Most would fold in less than a year.

"You want to try rolling with me again?" he asked.

I smiled.

"Absolutely, and don't you dare take it easy on me."

Dillon smiled back.

"I won't."

Fight For Me 19

We started on our knees on the mat. We slapped hands and then Dillon shot in. I was ready for him this time and caught him in what I thought was a tight guillotine. I hooked his inner thighs with my feet and tried to use the guillotine and the momentum of his shot to flip him onto his back, but he managed to maintain his balance and thwart my reversal attempt. Now, he was on top of me.

I still had the choke hold, but I could feel his head slipping out. I squeezed for all I was worth but couldn't tap him. He had his chin tucked between my arm and his throat, lessening the pressure just enough to keep me from rendering him unconscious. He had both hands on my arm, pushing down as he pulled his head out. Then, he was free, and he had me mounted. I had no illusions about being able to easily dislodge him from the mount. I knew I was fucked. But I wasn't about to give up. If he was going to beat me this time, I was going to make it much harder for him.

He was riding high, straddling my chest. I could feel the outline of his cock through his shorts. It was pressed right between my breasts, and I had a momentary flash of disappointment when I noticed that he wasn't hard. But of course he wasn't. We were supposed to be fighting, not fucking. I was supposed to be trying to get out of this position, not waiting for him to tit-fuck me.

My first thought was to give up my back and try to slip out between his legs, but that's how I'd gotten choked out the last time. He'd shown me a few defenses, but I wasn't confident enough that they would work. I hadn't exactly mastered them yet.

As I laid there, trying to decide what to do, Dillon popped me on the side of the head with an open palm. These playful slaps took the place of real punches in the gym during a friendly sparring session, but they let me know that, had he wanted to, he could have clocked me with a solid punch instead of that little slap. He popped me again. It was time to make a move.

Instead of trying to buck him off or slip out between his legs like I'd tried and failed before, I swung my legs up and wrapped them around his chest, then flipped him backwards and off of me. I was surprised it worked. Then, when I saw Dillon grinning at me, nodding his head in approval, I realized he'd let me do it.

"I said, don't take it easy on me!"

"It was a good move," Dillon said.

"Bullshit. That shouldn't have worked. That was a white belt move and you're ..."

"A black belt. But that doesn't mean anything. Anyone can get caught."

"But you didn't get caught. That was way too easy. You're not fooling me. Now, stop fucking around and let's fight!" I said. Yeah, I was a little pissed. I didn't want a Jiu Jitsu lesson. We'd already done that. I wanted a real fight. I wanted to conquer or be conquered.

We rolled for another thirty minutes, and this time, Dillon didn't give me an inch. He tapped me about a dozen times. Arm bars, leg locks, and about six different chokes. I wanted to be conquered, and I was. Thoroughly. But I was also learning a lot. Enough to know that I would be Dillon's equal long before I got my black belt. When he reversed my clumsy attempt at an arm bar and mounted me again, I placed both of his hands on my neck and whispered:

"Choke me." Then I reached down between his legs, feeling for his cock.

He stiffened in my hands. I reached inside and pulled his cock out, stroking it. He looked around in a panic.

Fight For Me 21

"What are you doing? The rest of the guys will be here any minute. Coach could walk in."

"He's back there in his office doing paperwork. He won't walk in. Besides, the threat of getting caught is half the fun. Now, choke me."

I licked my palm, using my saliva to lubricate his cock as I continued jacking him off. His hands tightened around my neck. The harder he squeezed, the faster I stroked him. Then I reached down and pulled off my own shorts.

"Fuck me," I wheezed. He didn't need to be told twice. He slid between my legs and rammed his engorged cock deep inside me. I gasped as he continued choking me while he fucked me hard. I thrust my hips up to meet each stroke, urging him deeper, harder. I was starting to see spots. I began struggling to get free.

"Are you okay? You want me to stop?" Dillon asked.

"No. I want you to take it. I want you to fight me for it."

And he did. I tried to push him away and he held on, riding me like a wild horse. I fought the hands around my throat as I began to lose consciousness. Dillon grabbed me by the wrist with one hand while continuing to choke me with the other. And then, I erupted.

My body bucked and convulsed as the orgasm took it over. He came too. His body stiffened and I could feel him filling me with his seed. He collapsed on top of me. Spent and exhausted. It had been quick, but intense. Rough, angry, violent sex. Just what I had been needing.

I rolled him off of me and pulled up my shorts. He just barely managed to pull his shorts up before the first of the fighters walked through the door. I rolled well that night, better than I ever had. I even managed to tap Dillon once, though that was probably unfair. Needless to say, he was a bit distracted.

5

I didn't show up early the next day, but I did stay late. Dillon stayed too. That wasn't unusual. He had a key to the gym and usually locked up for coach at the end of the night. Dillon had been watching me all night as I rolled and sparred with everyone but him. I was playing hard to get, and it was working.

Finally, there were only three of us left in the gym. Me, Dillon, and a Brazilian light heavyweight named Armando who I'd sparred with a few times before. Armando was young, well-built, with dark curly hair, tan skin, and beautiful almond eyes. He had come to America to train with our coach and had dreams of a big-time fighting career. He was over six-foot which, as shallow as it sounds, already made him more attractive than Dillon.

I rolled with both of them, one at a time. They were both strong and talented. I couldn't beat either of them, but I learned from both. And, I had to admit, getting manhandled by Armando was sexy as hell. I decided to throw caution to the wind.

"I want to watch you two fight," I said.

Dillon shook his head.

"It's getting late. I've been training all day."

I smiled at him.

"The winner gets a blow job."

Both of them looked stunned, so stunned that I had to laugh.

"Oh, you're just joking," Armando said.

"I'm not joking at all. You beat Dillon, and I'll suck your cock."

Armando's smile widened. It was a beautiful smile.

"How about if I beat Dillon, you suck my cock, and let me fuck you."

"Deal."

"In your ass," Armando said, locking eyes with me. Daring me.

"Deal," I repeated.

"What if I don't want to fight him?" Dillon asked.

"Then you don't get to fuck me."

Dillon thought about it for a second, then started wrapping his hands. I could hardly contain my excitement.

"No rounds. MMA rules. You fight until one of you taps or gets knocked out."

"You're crazy," Dillon said.

"And you're horny. And you know how good this pussy is. Well, my mouth is just as good."

They both finished wrapping their hands, put on their MMA gloves and mouthpieces, and walked into the cage. I was so wet, I couldn't keep my hands off of myself. So I didn't. I took my shirt off, letting my D-cup breasts hang loose. Both Dillon and Armando stopped to stare, their mouths fell open and their eyes widened like a kid on Christmas morning. It reminded me of a joke I heard once. "Why don't women with double D breasts go to the gym?

Because they don't have to." A woman with big breasts didn't need very much else to get a man. That had always been my ace in the hole. But, I realized fairly early in life, and was reminded again after finally getting rid of the loser I was married to, that if a woman wanted a better quality of man, she had to use more than just her tits. When I thought about it, Dillon had never actually seen my breasts before, either. I hadn't taken my shirt off when I let him fuck me on the mat the day before. And poor Armando acted like he'd never seen a pair of tits in his life. He was practically drooling.

"Wow," they said in unison.

"Get ready to rumble, boys," I said as I slid a hand down between my legs and began to rub my clit. The two of them tapped gloves. The fight was on.

So, I know, this was all very brazen of me. I was acting like a cock-hungry whore. But I had never had a chance to act this way. My best years, when I should have been hitting the nightclubs, getting drunk, and having one-night stands with hot college jocks, I had been in a relationship and then a marriage. I'd had to listen to all of my friends' tales of sexual excess while I was the faithful and dutiful wife. Even the evenings they regretted sounded better than my most romantic evenings with my ex-husband, Steve. Now it was time to live out a few fantasies. I was finally discovering myself. I refused to be embarrassed by my own desires, no matter how unusual they might be. I wasn't about to slut-shame myself.

Armando threw a head-kick immediately, trying to end the fight as quickly as possible, but Dillon easily blocked it and answered with a roundhouse kick to the body and a jab, right-cross, left hook combination followed by a knee to Armando's belly that startled him. Obviously, he hadn't expected Dillon to be so aggressive. Neither had I. And, even though I knew Dillon was just a naturally competitive guy, I kept telling myself that he was fighting harder because he really wanted me, which excited the hell out of me. Every girl wants to feel wanted, desired. And having two guys beat the hell out of each other for you was about as desired as a woman could feel.

They stood toe-toe, trading punches and leg and body kicks in the center of the cage. Armando caught Dillon with a right hook to the body followed by a right uppercut and a left hook. Dillon answered with a double left hook to the body and head, followed by an overhand right that landed flush on Armando's jaw. Armando threw a right roundhouse kick to Dillon's ribs and a left hook, straight right combination. Then Dillon threw a right leg kick, right body kick, right head kick combination. All three kicks landed and Armando wobbled, momentarily dazed. Then Dillon shot in for a take down, but Armando sprawled and stuffed Dillon's face right into the canvas. Dillon popped back up and received an elbow to the forehead that opened up a nasty gash that gushed blood all down his face.

"Dude, you're bleeding." Armando said.

"You quitting? Cause I ain't," Dillon answered, and threw a straight right to Armando's belly.

I was masturbating furiously while watching the two gladiators battle it out. I had taken my shorts completely off along with my panties and was fucking myself with three fingers shoved deep inside me and my other hand rubbing my clit. I came three times as Dillon and Armando traded blows, splattering the mat with their blood.

As Dillon tried for the single-leg take down, Armando caught him right on the chin with a flying knee that sent Dillon to the canvas hard. It looked like he wasn't going to

Fight For Me

get up, but when Armando jumped on top of him and began raining down punches, Dillon pulled him into his guard, swiveled his hips to the left, wrapped one of his legs around the back of Armando's neck while controlling one of the young Brazilian's right arms. He then hooked his other leg around his own ankle and pulled Armando's head down, cinching a tight triangle choke.

I could see the panic in Armando's eyes and then the rage and determination that replaced it. Choking, gasping for air, looking like he would pass out at any minute, Armando lifted Dillon right off the mat, over his head, arching his back to get his opponent as high as he could before slamming him back down to the canvas on his head. Dillon's head whipped backwards, striking the canvas hard and knocking him unconscious. Armando landed a couple hard hammer fists before he realized Dillon wasn't responding.

"He's out! Dillon's out! Stop hitting him!" I yelled, and Armando stopped. He was still kneeling over his unconscious training partner when I opened the gate and ran into the cage to make sure Dillon was okay. I was still naked, and Armando stared at my breasts with undisguised lust while they bounced and swayed as I bounded into the cage and knelt down beside the two fighters.

"Dillon! Are you okay?"

Slowly, Dillon's eyes opened and he rose to a sitting position.

"Take it easy, bro. You took some hard shots. Just sit there for a few minutes. I'll go get you some water," Armando said.

"What happened? Did I get choked out?"

"Nope. You got knocked out. You had me in a triangle

choke, and I slammed you on your head, Rampage Jackson style. You were out cold, bro."

"Damn! I can't believe you beat me!"

Armando shrugged, smiling wide.

"Everybody loses sometime."

He left the cage and went to get Dillon some water. Dillon's face was so sad I almost wanted to fuck him anyway. He had fought hard. But Armando had won. It wouldn't have been fair to deny him his prize.

"Are you really going to fuck Armando?" Dillon asked.

I nodded.

"Oh, you better believe I am. To the victor goes the spoils. Besides, that was really fucking hot."

"Well, I'll get him next time."

"How do you know there will be a next time?" I asked with a coy little smirk.

"Oh, there better be."

But that was the last night I ever fucked any of the guys at the gym.

6

WE CALLED A RIDE-HAILING SERVICE FOR DILLON, NOT trusting him to drive after getting his brain scrambled. We tried to talk him into going to the hospital to get checked out, to make sure he didn't have a concussion, but he wasn't having it.

"Of course I have a concussion. I just got knocked out. But all they're going to do at the hospital is put a bag of ice on my head, give me some ibuprofen, and watch me to make sure I don't slip into a coma or something. My sister can do that for me without charging me thousands of dollars for it. I just want to go home and lick my wounds."

Dillon's ride came, and Armando and I helped him into the car. We waited until the driver was out of sight before going back into the gym.

"So, your place or mine?" Armando said, grinning from ear to ear.

"Right here. There's just one more thing you have to do."

"Oh, and what's that?"

"You have to fight me for it."

"What?"

"I didn't stutter."

I turned my back to him and walked back into the cage. Armando was right behind me.

"You seriously want me to fight you?"

"If you want this pussy, you have to take it."

"Uh uh. It's not your pussy I want. You promised me a blow job and that I get to fuck you in the ass. That's what I want."

I nodded slowly. What had I gotten myself into?

"If you beat me, you can have whatever you want."

When Armando shot in for a double-leg take down, easily dragging me to the mat, I knew I would be sucking his cock soon. Because of his size, I was even less of a match for Armando then I had been for Dillon.

Armando had none of the reservations about hurting a woman that Dillon had. He tossed me around like a rag doll, mounted me, and slapped me hard across the face.

"You give up?"

"Slap me again," I said.

"You are crazy," he said, smiling wide, his gorgeous almond eyes twinkling mischievously. I could see the outline of his erection through his shorts as it swelled. He was bigger than Dillon in more than one way. He slapped me again, harder this time, then he took out his cock and forced it between my lips. I sucked it obediently. He had beaten me, just like I wanted him to, and sucking his long thick cock was his reward and my pleasure.

Armando began thrusting his cock in and out of my mouth, hitting the back of my throat and testing my gag reflex as he fucked my face. My head banged against the mat with each thrust, and I was almost dizzy when he finally exploded in my mouth, filling it with his seed until it overflowed and spilled down my cheeks.

Fight For Me

"Keep sucking it," Armando said. "Get me hard again."

And so I did. I licked the underside of his cock, licked and sucked his balls, then slid his cock as far down my throat as I could manage. I repeated those motions a few more times before he was hard again.

"Roll over," he said. When I refused, he wrestled me onto my belly, easily overcoming my token resistance. I lubed up his thumb with my saliva, and he slid it between my ass cheeks, into my anus, pumping it in and out until I loosened up. Then he withdrew it, and I felt the head of his cock nudge its way in. I grunted as his full length slowly filled me. He had one arm wrapped tightly around my throat and the other pinning my wrists together above my head as he began to speed up the rhythm of his thrusts. He fucked me hard as I struggled beneath him. When I stopped struggling and relaxed, enjoying this new invasion, he let go of my wrists and reached beneath me to find my sex, which was now sopping wet. He slid two fingers inside me while rubbing my clitoris with his thumb.

He was thrusting harder now, pounding my virgin ass while he played with my pussy and I moaned and grunted. It wasn't long before I felt his body stiffen, his cock swell inside of me, before he filled my ass with his seed. I came again then too.

The next day, I switched gyms.

This gym had now been compromised. It had been stupid of me to fuck one, now two of the fighters. I would never be taken seriously here now, and I still wanted to train. I found a new gym and took my newly discovered kink online. I put an ad on an adult dating site that said:

Fight For Me. Real fighters wanted to compete for a chance to fuck me. My photos are below. You must beat all of your competi-

tors, and then, you must defeat me. The winner gets to fuck me any way they like.

I posted several nude photos, posed as provocatively as I could without being completely pornographic. Not that it would have mattered on this site where men and women regularly posted photos and videos of themselves having sex. But, I wanted to seem more mysterious, untouchable. That would make them want me more. It only took a few hours before I began getting responses.

7

"YOU DID WHAT?" BECCA ASKED. SHE WAS BLOW DRYING A client's hair, but she had heard me perfectly. I could tell by the grin on her face.

"I know. I'm such a harlot."

"A harlot? No, dear. You're a slut," Becca laughed.

"But not a whore," I said, laughing.

"No. Definitely not a whore. A whore would have made good money doing what you did for free."

The salon was bustling. I had a new client, a referral from Marie Claire. Gypsy Lane. She was an internet porn star, famous for lesbian breastfeeding videos. She apparently made good money doing it. I charged six-hundred dollars for a dye and cut.

"Well, it sounds pretty damn hot to me. You'd be a millionaire if you'd filmed it and sold it on the internet. Two hot guys fighting over you, with you fucking the winner? I'm getting wet just thinking about it," Gypsy said.

"See, now *she's* a whore," Becca said.

"Dyke," Gypsy retorted.

"And a damn good one," Becca replied, making a V with

two fingers and flicking her tongue in and out between them.

"No calling my new client a whore, please,"

Gypsy laughed.

"That's okay. I am a whore," Gypsy said. "And a damn good one. I'd give her something to do with that tongue."

Gypsy winked at Becca, who blushed as her face lit up with a goofy smile.

I had told Becca all about making Dillon and Armando fighting for me and how I fucked Armando right there in the cage. The salon was busy today. All ten chairs were occupied. Becca and I were two of only four women who worked at the exclusive salon. Of the six guys who worked there, two were straight, and they were serious competition. Perfect hair, perfect teeth, tanned, Cross-fit bodies. A good looking, straight, male hair designer was worth his weight in gold. They snatched up most of the desperate housewives, leaving the rest of us to fight for what was left. Luckily, Jake and Mike could only take on so many clients at a time or the rest of us would have been broke.

"You sure you aren't going just a little crazy? I mean, it's only been a few months since your divorce. Maybe you should slow down," Becca said.

I frowned at her.

"Seriously, Becca? You're telling me to slow down? How many women did you sleep with last weekend?"

Becca opened her mouth to protest, then quickly shut it.

"Okay. Good point. But, in my defense, it was Memorial Day weekend and I was DJing at a nightclub."

"Uh huh. So that means you had a lot of opportunity, and you went for it. Well, I was in a gym surrounded by big, sweaty, muscular, alpha males secreting testosterone through their pores like a pheromone."

Fight For Me

35

"Shit! I would have fucked both of them," Angelica said. She was one of the only clients I had that was around my age. Her husband was fifteen years older than her and owned two upscale Mexican food restaurants. One in the financial district, and one in the trendier section of the Mission District.

"My husband is an old man. I mean, I love him, but he can't always get it up when I want it, you know? If I was single, raslin' on the floor with a bunch of big hunky guys, I'd let them fuck me. I think that shit is sexy as fuck. What? It's true. I would. I'm so horny I'd even go to Becca's nightclub and pick up a woman."

Becca shook her head.

"Bitches are crazy."

"Oh, Becca. You know you'd fuck me."

Becca was about to rip into Angelica when I gave her a look, begging her to let it slide. Angelica was a regular, and I wasn't cheap. I didn't want to lose a good client because Becca couldn't take a joke.

"What you should do," Angelica said, "is put an ad on Jane's List. Fight For Me, winner takes all. You'll have guys lining up to throw down for a chance to get some pussy."

"Don't you dare encourage her," Becca said. But it was too late, the seed had been planted, and the idea wasn't without its appeal.

"You think guys would really do that?"

Both Becca and Angelica now looked at me like I was crazy.

"Are you kidding me? You would have every muscle-bound meathead from every gym in this city lining up. You'd have to make a tournament out of it."

I saw Becca looking at me. She was reading my face. She had known me much too long, much too well.

"You aren't really considering doing it, are you?"

"Oh, come on, Becca. If it was girls all fighting for you, wouldn't you think that was hot as hell? Don't tell me you wouldn't."

"Yeah, but girls aren't guys."

"No, sometimes they're worse."

"True, but at least I can kick their asses if they try anything stupid. You're talking about the type of guys who beat the hell out of other guys. What if they try to take things further than you want to go? What if they get rough with you?"

"I want them to get rough with me."

"No, I mean really rough. I'm serious. This sounds really dangerous."

"Well, it's just a thought. I didn't say I was going to do it."

Becca frowned and raised an eyebrow.

"I didn't just meet you yesterday. I know damn well you're going to do it."

"Okay." I looked around slyly. "I kind of already put out an ad. Not on Jane's List. On an adult site. I just wanted to see if anyone would respond. I haven't worked out the details yet. I'm trying to think of a way to do it that will keep me safe."

Becca wore an expression that was simultaneously worried. skeptical, and slightly pissed-the-fuck-off.

"How many guys answered your ad?" Becca asked.

"A couple dozen. Not many of them were really fighters, though. Only a handful. I haven't written any of them back."

"And are you going to?"

"Ooh! You have to! You have to do it! That would be so fucking hot!" Angelica squealed.

"I think you might be right," I said, thinking of all the possibilities. "Fuck it. I'm doing it."

Fight For Me

Becca's mouth dropped open.

"Seriously?"

"Seriously. I mean, what have I got to lose?"

"Your dignity. Your self-respect. Maybe even some teeth or even your life," Becca replied.

"You're being melodramatic."

"Am I?"

"Yes. It's no different than those girls who arrange to meet a bunch of strange guys they found on Jane's List in hotel rooms for gang bangs."

"You're right! It isn't any different. It's just as fucking stupid and dangerous."

"But yet women do it all the time. There are adult meet up sites all over the place just for women who want to get gang banged by a bunch of strange men, usually with their husbands or boyfriends filming the whole thing."

"Yeah, at least their husbands are there in case something goes wrong. Maybe I should be there when you meet these guys?" Becca said. "I'm the one who was a kickboxing champion. You just look intimidating. I can actually back it up."

I rolled my eyes. The last thing I wanted was for Becca to see me like ... that. The wanton slut I was when watching big, muscular, aggressive, alpha males fight over me. The crazy submissive thing I became once a man was able to subdue me.

"First, how long has it been since you've trained? Like four or five years?"

"Three and a half."

"Second, you're smaller than I am. These guys will probably all be huge."

"You hope they are. But, just like your friend Dillon, I

don't have to be big to be dangerous. I can kick most men's asses without breaking a sweat."

"And third, I have been training. And I'm getting pretty good. I can take care of myself."

"You've never even had a real fight, Athena. Sparring and actually fighting someone who is trying to rip your head off are two different things. You need me there. Guys will be less likely to try anything funny if you aren't alone."

How could I tell her that the danger was all part of it? The threat of actual physical harm? Being vulnerable to a man for once in my life?

All my life, I have been the big girl. I was the tallest girl in every grade right up until high school, and even then, most guys had only wanted those little petite girls, which I was not. Even my dad treated me more like a son than his little girl. He never worried about me the way fathers were supposed to worry about their daughters.

"I know you can handle yourself," he'd always say, and that "knowledge" was based solely on my physical stature.

It wasn't until my senior year that I embraced my size and learned to love it. That's when I joined both the power-lifting team and the wrestling team, and made it to the state finals in both. If I hadn't started so late, if I'd had one more year to compete, I was confident I would have won medals. Still, athletic talents aside, being a female powerlifter and wrestler hadn't made me any more desirable to the opposite sex. Except the ones with a fetish for being dominated.

I attracted submissive freaks like flies. They took one look at me and fell all over themselves to bow at my feet. Even the ones who came on all macho and in command at first were quick to yield control over to me once we were in a relationship. Eventually, I gave the whole BDSM scene a try. What choice did I have? The men I wanted didn't want

Fight For Me   39

me, or couldn't handle me. And the men who did want me all wanted to be my slave. At six foot, one hundred and eighty pounds, covered in black latex and leather from head to toe, I looked every bit the part of the stern dominatrix, and it turned out I was good at it too. I learned intricate rope bondage, how to crack a whip, wield a cane or a paddle, and florentine with two floggers like I was twirling batons. But my specialty was humiliation. I could make any man feel like the worthless piece of shit I feared all men were.

Becca got me a job at a dungeon working as a pro-Domme. That was how I paid my way through beauty school, but it also lowered my impression of men even more, convincing me that the type of strong, dominant man I was looking for was a mythological creature only found in chick-flicks, action thrillers, and romance novels. That all men secretly wanted a woman to humble them. They were only good for opening their wallets and kissing my boots. My marriage to Steve had only confirmed my opinion of men as weak, helpless things.

Steve had been my bitch through our entire marriage, and he still was. Becca called him my own personal vibrator. We had been divorced for a year, yet I still called him up from time to time to come over and lick my pussy when I really needed a release. Then, the minute I reached my climax, I would tell him to leave, denying him an orgasm. That's all I thought men were good for, that is, until I walked into that MMA gym. Until Dillon choked me almost unconscious. Now I had found what I'd always wanted, and I didn't want to share it with anyone. Not even my best friend.

"I don't know. This is kind of ... personal."

"Personal? You just told the entire salon that you put an ad online for men to fight for your pussy."

"Yeah, but saying it is one thing. You being there ... I don't know. It just feels like it would be weird."

It was an irrational thing. I knew. The last thing Becca would ever be interested in were big sweaty men. But, I still felt jealous about sharing this discovery with her. It was like I had found my own Shangri-La valley in that gym, in those fighters, and letting anyone else in would somehow tarnish this paradise. All Becca would have to say is one disparaging word, cast one disapproving gaze upon the proceedings, and the beautiful illusion would be forever sullied.

"Zero judgment. I promise. I'll just be there for your protection," Becca said, holding her hands up in the universal gesture of harmlessness. It was as if she could read my mind.

I narrowed my eyes at her. The frown on my face conveyed all my reservations as well as the warning I had yet to voice.

Don't make me regret this.

"Okay, Becca. But zero judgment."

"I promise," Becca replied, drawing an "X" across her heart with her fingertip. "But, I have one more request ..."

I sighed, wondering how far Becca was going to push this thing before I told her to fuck off and just did the thing myself, consequences be damned.

"What now, Becca?"

"You're going to want to fight them too, right? Whoever wins the tournament? You aren't just going to throw your legs up in the air for the winner without a struggle. I know you better than that. You're going to want the winner to prove himself against you. So, let me train you for that. I was an amateur champion, but I trained with a lot of pros. If I didn't like drinking and fucking so much, I might have turned pro myself. I know my shit. I may not know all those

Fight For Me

grappling moves, but I can teach you how to kick ass standing up. You'll just have to find another Jujitsu coach."

I nodded.

"Okay, deal."

I was actually happy at the thought of her training me to fight some mystery man for the right to claim me as his. It turned the whole thing into a project for us girls. That night, while we sat in our pajamas, drinking chardonnay and eating chocolate, Becca and I crafted my new ad on Jane's List:

Fight For Me

I am a 6 foot redhead. My measurements are 36", 31", 40". My bra size is DD. So, if you like petite women, I am not for you. But, if you are man enough for a real amazon warrior princess, I can be yours. All you have to do is fight for me. I am talking about a No Holds Barred fighting tournament. The winner gets me as his sex slave for one night, maybe more. Text me for more information.

WE WERE BOTH DRUNK, GIGGLING LIKE SCHOOLGIRLS AS WE wrote the ad. Once I pressed send, and it all became real, I was terrified.

"Oh, no. What the fuck did I just do?"

"Don't worry, babe. I'll make sure no one hurts you," Becca said. And I knew she would, but what if no one answered the ad? What if someone did?

"I'm so nervous I think I'm going to wet myself."

"That's because we just drank two bottles of wine."

"Make that three," I said, uncorking a bottle of Cabernet

We had just filled our glasses when Becca's phone rang, startling us both. Getting phone calls had become unusual. Everyone we knew texted, at the least they texted first and then called. Getting an unexpected phone call was never good.

Becca answered the phone on the third ring. I could hear the sound of someone sobbing on the other end of the phone. Death in the family? Broken-hearted lover? Then I saw the expression on Becca's face go from concerned, to worried, to furious, and I knew.

"When are they releasing you? You sure you shouldn't stay overnight for observation? It damn sure sounds serious to me. And where's Manuel? Is he in jail? Well, why the fuck not?"

"Trish?" I asked, already knowing the answer.

Becca nodded.

"Did he hit her again?"

She nodded again, with her mouth twisted in a nasty scowl.

"How bad?"

Becca covered the phone with her hand and whispered.

"She's at the hospital. She has a broken nose and a concussion. And ..."

"And what? What else did he do?"

"He raped her. Anally."

"Oh my God! Did she press charges?"

Becca rolled her eyes and shook her head. I felt the anger rise in me like some dark, violent, living thing crawling up from my belly into my chest. I wanted to hit something, to destroy something. I wanted to beat the shit out of Manuel.

"Tell her to meet you over here."

"Meet me?"

"Yeah, I'm going to see Manuel," I said, already putting my shoes on and looking for my keys.

Becca held up her hand, signaling for me to wait.

Fight For Me

43

"Trish? Athena and I are coming to the hospital to pick you up. You wait right there for us. You're going to spend the rest of the night with us. Just us girls. Like old times. Don't worry about it, we'll let Manuel know we're getting you, and that he shouldn't bother. Who gives a fuck if he gets mad? He's damn lucky he isn't in jail where his ass should be. No arguments, Trish. We're coming to get you in one hour."

Becca hung up the phone and turned to look at me with murder in her eyes.

"This shit stops tonight."

"Let's go," I replied.

Trish was a girl we used to party with. We'd met her in beauty school and had kept in touch over the years. She was the thin, pretty, petite model type that guys always went for. Traditionally beautiful, without the blonde hair or the blue eyes. Trish's dad was African American and her mother was German. Her parents met in Germany when her dad was still in the military. She was born there and lived there for the first eight years of her life. Her family moved to the Bay Area once her dad retired.

Before becoming a hairstylist, Trish had tried everything from modeling to acting to working as a stripper. Doing whatever she could to capitalize on her stunning looks. She had brown curly hair, smooth light brown skin, green eyes, thick pouty lips, and long, coltish legs. People said she looked like a young Janet Jackson. She was always dressed stylish and sexy, maxing out credit cards to fill her closets with the latest designer labels. She was, basically, everything I wasn't.

When we used to go out to the nightclubs together, guys fell all over themselves trying to impress her, and she always left the nightclub with the best looking guy in the joint. Two years ago, that guy had been Manuel. Half Puerto-Rican, half Italian. Built like Brad Pitt, but with the dark smoldering eyes and handsome Latin features of a young Antonio Banderas. He'd laid the charm on thick, buying drinks for both me and Trish and showering us with compliments. It didn't hurt that he was also an exceptional dancer. There was no way Trish was going to let him get away. They had been dating ever since. They'd moved in together after they'd only been dating for four months, and the emotional and physical abuse had begun soon afterward.

"Are you sure this is the right thing to do? I mean, what if it only makes things worse for Trish? You know she's not going to leave him."

"He can't keep getting away with abusing women. We have to do something. If Trish won't press charges, what else can we do? Besides, he needs his ass kicked!"

"No argument from me there," Becca replied.

8

——————

Tyrell sat in his hotel room, reading a horror novel. Supernatural terrors took his mind off his own fucked up life. The bloodier the novels, the greater the escapism worked. And this one was as gruesome as it got. It was a novel about a family of inbred cannibals living in an urban ghetto and a bunch of white kids out slumming it in the hood who get trapped in their house. It was by an author named Brian Keene. Tyrell had read a couple zombie novels by this author before. He liked the guy's style. He was a white dude who could write about black folks without making them all sound like they stepped out of a Snoop Dogg video. Tyrell was just getting to a really nasty part when his cell phone rang.

"About damn time," he growled, as he answered the phone. It was Byrd.

"There will be a car waiting for you downstairs in ten minutes. There will be an envelope on the back seat. That's your meal. The driver will take you to dinner."

The phone call ended, and Tyrell scowled at it. He hated that cryptic shit. The paranoid fuck on the other end of the phone had been setting up jobs for Tyrell for the last fifteen years, and he always acted like they were on a goddamned spy mission instead of just taking out some piece of garbage that probably deserved the very worst end Tyrell could conceive of for him. But, Tyrell had to admit, you never knew who might be listening in on your conversations these days. The fucking terrorists had fucked it up for everyone. Now, Homeland Security, FBI, CIA, and who the hell knew who else could be listening in. All in the name of keeping America safe. It made everything that much harder for honest psychopaths like himself.

Tyrell stood and stretched his long, muscular frame. He picked up a black suitcase and checked its contents. Two .40 caliber Sig Sauer semi-automatic pistols and four high-capacity magazines, along with a ten-inch long, carbonized steel, Japanese tanto knife. This would be more than enough for the meal tonight, even if there were any surprises, and Tyrell secretly hoped there would be. The client was paying for a clean hit. But Tyrell was getting bored with clean and professional. He was in the mood for something brutal and messy.

He shrugged into his dual shoulder holster, placed a gun under each arm, picked up the tanto knife, placing it in a sheath that hung between his shoulder blades, then put on his black blazer. He switched on several Wi-Fi cameras he'd strategically placed around the room, then made sure his cell phone was receiving the signal. The cameras had built-in motion detectors and would turn on and start recording the instant anyone passed in front of one. That recording was then relayed live to his phone as a video call. Anyone sets foot in that hotel room, and Tyrell would know about it.

Tyrell's hotel room was at the very back of the posh building on the second floor. Low enough to the ground for him to jump out a window if he needed to. Tyrell didn't trust elevators either. He'd seen one too many good guys ambushed in elevators. He took the stairs down and walked out of an emergency exit. Paranoia kept you alive.

A nondescript black sedan waited for him in the alley. The driver, an old black man who'd probably been chauffeuring criminals around town for various mob bosses since before Tyrell had been born, greeted him with a nod and held the door open for him. Tyrell returned the nod and slipped into the back seat. As promised, a large manilla envelope waited for him. Tyrell opened the envelope and began reading its contents and committing the photo to memory as the car pulled out of the alley and made its way through the busy downtown streets, taking Tyrell to his meal.

The "meal" was a lawyer. It didn't say why someone wanted him dead. It never did. But Tyrell could imagine a myriad of sins a crooked lawyer may have committed to get him on his hit list. He could imagine several dozen an honest lawyer might have committed. The photo showed a slim, young, good-looking, white guy with a fashionable haircut and a cocky grin. He had an apartment in North Beach that overlooked the water. He worked for a good law firm, but not a great one. Tyrell created an entire backstory for the guy that included fancy cars he couldn't really afford, cocaine, hookers, gambling, and doing illegal favors for the type of guys who hired men like Tyrell.

All the research had already been done for him, and Tyrell trusted the intel. Byrd knew what would happen if he gave him the wrong or incomplete information. He had a missing pinky to remind him. Tyrell hated the pre-work. He liked to get in and get out. That's why he'd hired an obsessive-compulsive tech-geek like Byrd to handle that part. It was Byrd's job to gather as much intel from the client as possible and double and triple check it all before accepting the job. He didn't negotiate price. It was a flat fee, and the client either paid that or found someone else. Once the job was accepted, he called Tyrell and made travel arrangements, including fake IDs, ground transportation, hotel, and weaponry. None of it traceable. For that, he got twenty-percent. If he fucked up any part of that, he might very well get a closed casket funeral, or a shallow grave in the desert. It was an arrangement that worked.

The car pulled up in front of a crisp, new, five story, white brick building with a doorman.

"Keep driving past, drive around back, and pull up on the other side of the building," Tyrell said. He wanted to verify all the exits Byrd had indicated. He trusted Byrd, but he wasn't an idiot. It would be his ass on the line if an exit was blocked or a guard had been posted, or some cop chose that night to park in the alley for a quick nap or a blow job from some street whore. The intel was 24-hours old, and a lot of things could change in a day.

All the exits were clear. There were three. One in the front. Last resort. One in the back, and one on the right side of the building that was attached to the kitchen. That was the second best choice. His plan involved sprinting down five flights of stairs and out the back door once he was done with his meal.

"One more time around," Tyrell said.

As they approached the front of the building, Tyrell spotted the meal coming out the front door with a scantily clad woman on his left arm and a big, six foot Italian guy, who weighed in excess of three hundred pounds (mostly fat), that Tyrell assumed was a bodyguard, flanking him on the right. He looked drunk, or high, or both, as did the girl.

Fight For Me

The bodyguard was laughing and joking right along with them and didn't seem to be taking the job very seriously. He didn't check the surroundings before leaving his client on the sidewalk and stepping out into the street to wave down a ride.

Either the lawyer was really bad and into shit that required him to employ a bodyguard, or he was a pompous asshole who hired a bodyguard as a status symbol. When the Cadillac Escalade limousine pulled up to the trio and they piled inside, Tyrell was pretty certain it was the latter. He'd probably hired the guy based on his size. Watching the way they laughed and joked with each other, Tyrell guessed they were friends. Byrd hadn't mentioned a bodyguard. Tyrell would have to have a long talk with the man about that oversight.

"Follow them."

The limo drove off, carrying the lawyer and his two friends. Fifteen seconds later, Tyrell's driver pulled away from the curb as well, following four cars behind. The limo made several stops, a liquor store, a rundown loft in the warehouse district that served as a meth and crack house, and a couple trendy nightclubs, before arriving at one of the more upscale gentleman's clubs. Tyrell rolled his eyes. This was probably where the lawyer had met both the girl and the muscle. They both fit the surroundings perfectly. Places like these tended to hire huge body-builder types as bouncers and half emaciated women with big fake tits as entertainment. This was the wrong place for a hit. The meal would have to wait.

"It's not going to happen tonight. Get Byrd on the phone and tell him what happened. Let him know we need new intel. Maybe we'll try again tomorrow night. Also ... tell him I am not happy."

While the driver made the call, Tyrell thought of all the ways he would make Byrd suffer for his fuckup. He didn't want to kill the guy. He needed him, but he had to make him understand that this type of sloppiness could not be tolerated. It could not go unpunished. Maybe Byrd needed to lose another finger? This time, maybe he'd bite it off. He'd missed his opportunity to feed the beast, and now it was ravenous. He could feel the bloodlust growing within him like a cancer, infecting every cell, spreading like a virus. Killing that lawyer would have kept it at bay for weeks, longer if he'd made it bloody, but now it had been too long since he'd hurt someone. He needed his fix of violence.

"What is there to do in this town?" Tyrell asked the driver, interrupting his rather terse conversation.

The driver lowered the cell phone and looked back at Tyrell. His aged countenance gave the appearance of one who'd been both wizened and corrupted by decades of crime and vice. His smile was weary, with the hopeless, tragic lack of enthusiasm of a junkie whose tolerance had grown to the point where he could no longer get high, but merely staved off sickness. This man seemed to have grown a tolerance to happiness itself. Tyrell wondered what it said of himself that he could relate. He was only truly happy when he was causing others pain, when he let the beast out and sated himself on blood, violence, and viscera.

"Depends on what you're looking for. Music? Alcohol? Drugs? Women? Boys?"

"Ask Byrd. He knows what I need. Tell him, if he finds me something good, I'll forget his little mistake tonight."

The driver nodded and began speaking into the cell phone.

"One sec. He's looking. He said to tell you he was sorry, and that he's grateful you're giving him another chance."

Fight For Me 51

Tyrell scowled.

"Tell him not to be grateful yet, and whatever he finds me better be damn good."

The driver relayed the message. A few minutes went by.

"He found something. He said it'll be even better than that bar full of white supremacist bikers. He's sending it to your cell phone."

Tyrell remembered that bar. That was a day when Tyrell had been out of control. The bloodlust had been unusually intense, and Byrd located a bunch of assholes that needed to be hurt. A racist biker group called The Windigos who'd recently been implicated in the beating and lynching of a gay black teenager. Tyrell had hurt them -- badly. It had helped a lot.

The cellphone vibrated. Tyrell answered it and found the text message. It was a copy of a personal ad from Jane's List.

"What the fuck is this? I'm not looking for a fucking date!"

The driver winced. He'd been around enough to know that it was not a good thing when men like Tyrell were unhappy. He quickly relayed Tyrell's displeasure to Byrd. He didn't know how right he was to be nervous. Tyrell was already sizing up the old black man as his next meal.

"He said to read it," the driver said.

Tyrell read through it and slowly began to smile.

"Okay, tell Byrd he gets to keep his other pinky."

Tyrell picked up his cell phone and texted the woman in the ad.

How do I get in on your tournament?

9

———

"You don't even know what that bitch said to me," Manuel said, waving us off dismissively as we stood in the entryway of the apartment he shared with Trish.

"Said to you? Said to you? You broke her fucking jaw! I don't give a fuck if she said she'd been in a gang bang with your father, brother, and best friend, you don't hit a woman!"

Manuel scowled.

"You know what, fuck you! This is none of your goddamn business."

I threw the first punch without even thinking about it. The blow landed square on Manuel's jaw. It staggered him, but didn't drop him.

"Fucking bitch! You want to fight like a man? I'll fight you like a man."

He took a step forward, and I felt a brief moment of fear. This was real, and like Becca had said, I had never been in a real fight, with someone really trying to hurt me, since high school. And I'd never been in a fight with a grown man. Becca stepped forward, brushing me out of the way, and thrusted a push-kick into Manuel's well-sculpted abdomen, driving all the wind out of his lungs and doubling him over. Then she cracked him with an elbow in a slashing downward strike which opened a gash over his cheek that immediately began to bleed.

Manuel dropped to one knee, but then he grabbed Becca by the waist and tried to drag her to the floor with him while Becca hammered him with elbows and hammerfists, trying to get him off of her. Manuel didn't let go, wrestling Becca off her feet and managing to get on top of her and pin her beneath him. He raised his fists to strike her, to pummel Becca as she lay trapped, helpless beneath his weight. Becca glowered at him without fear, eyes bristling with rage as she squirmed beneath him, struggling to free herself.

"Get the fuck off me, motherfucker!"

Manuel grinned, and instead of punching her, he slapped her across the face with the back of his hand, the way abusive men always hit women. The way he'd probably struck Trish countless times. Then he balled up his fists and prepared to punch her. That's when I snapped out of it and dove in, dragging him off her and tackling him to the ground.

I quickly took his back and wrapped my legs around his waist, trapping one arm as I tucked my right foot behind my left knee, putting his torso in a figure-four leg lock. With my hands free, I punched and elbowed the back of his head, his jaw, temple, raining down strikes, determined to do the most damage I possibly could.

"Get off of me! I'll fucking kill you, bitch!"

He turned his head to the right when he spoke, trying to get a good look at me while simultaneously trying to avoid my left hook. His neck was exposed now, so I took it,

Fight For Me

55

sliding my left arm beneath his chin and then locking it in place in the crook of my elbow. With my right arm, I pushed on the back of his head as I slid the choke in tighter, leaning back to stretch him out and tighten the choke even more.

"Achhhh! Uuuuurrrrrrl!"

He was still struggling, but I could feel him weakening. Becca stood above us. She kneeled down to look him in the eyes, then reached back and slapped the shit out of him, giving him the same pimp-slap he'd just given her. Then she balled up her fist and threw a right hook that crushed Manuel's nose and splashed blood and snot onto the entryway carpet. Manuel slumped against me, unconscious from either the choke hold or the punch. I held the choke a few seconds longer to make sure he was really unconscious. I squeezed even harder now than I had before, but he made no more sounds.

"Athena! Let him go before you kill him! He's out! Let him go!"

I released the choke, unwrapped my legs from around his torso, and allowed him to fall to the ground.

"What should we do with him?" I asked Becca. I was breathing heavy, but I felt good.

"We aren't done with this asshole," Becca replied, wiping blood from her split lip where Manuel had slapped her. It had already begun to swell. "We're going to do to him exactly what he did to Trish." Becca walked back over to the front door where she'd dropped her big striped Coach hand bag. She reached inside of it and pulled out a pair of hand-cuffs and a strap-on harness with a dildo attached to it that was every bit of ten inches long.

I couldn't help but laugh. It was exactly what that asshole deserved.

"Do you just carry that stuff around with you all the time?"

Becca shrugged.

"I had a date planned."

"But what if he calls the police? I don't want to go to jail."

"Call the police? And admit that he got his ass kicked and then got ass-raped by two chicks? You really think this macho asshole would do that? Come on."

"You're right. Hand me the handcuffs."

I cinched the cuffs in place around his wrists with his arms behind his back, then flipped him onto his belly and pulled off his pants and underwear.

"What happened? What's going on?" Manuel said groggily. "My throat hurts. I need some water."

Becca kicked him, or rather stomped him, in the side of his head twice. He fell unconscious again for twenty or thirty seconds, just long enough for her to finish strapping on the dildo and for me to grab a tub of margarine from the refrigerator, part his hairy ass-cheeks, and slather it onto his anus. That woke him up again. But now it was too late. I sat on his back to hold him in place while Becca lined up the huge dildo with his puckered rectum and slid it home with one merciless thrust.

"OWWW! Fuck! What the fuck are you bitches doing? Let me go! Nooo! Nooo! Heeeeeellllp!"

Becca was holding Manuel by the hips and ramming the dildo in and out with aggressive thrusts. He tore and bled and screamed. He cursed us, calling us bitches, dykes, whores, and threatened all manner of abuses upon us.

"You ever hurt Trish again, and I will make you choke on this dildo, you piece of shit!" Becca promised as she thrust even harder, splitting him open wider and drawing more blood. Manuel began to cry. We left him there, bleeding on

Fight For Me

the floor, curled into a fetal position and weeping. Becca threw him the keys to the handcuffs.

I grabbed him by the face and forced him to look at me. He was still blubbering and crying. He had been completely humbled.

"This is how Trish felt when you raped her. You remember this, because next time, we'll fucking kill you!"

Becca stood above him holding a smartphone. She snapped a photo of Manuel lying there handcuffed, pants around his ankles, bleeding from the ass.

"Smile for the camera."

"No! Don't!" He tried to squirm away as she took two more photos.

"You say anything about this to anyone and these photos hit the internet. You feel me?"

Manuel just glared at us.

"I need to hear you say it. Do you understand? Or, I can send them out right now. We've got a lot of the same friends. I can email all these photos directly. How about that?"

"I understand!"

"Good. I'm glad we understand each other," Becca said as we turned and walked out the door.

I was tempted to leave the apartment door open so the neighbors would find him there, deepening his embarrassment, but that would have probably put us in jeopardy too. Whoever found him would definitely call the cops. I closed the door ... mostly. This was San Francisco. There was the possibility that one of Manuel's more amorous and less scrupulous male neighbors might stumble across him in this vulnerable position and take advantage of it. I didn't want to deprive Manuel of that experience.

We arrived at the hospital twenty minutes later than we had promised, but Trish was only just beginning to get dressed when we knocked lightly on her hospital room door and stepped inside. Trish looked weak and frail, beaten deep inside. Her face was bruised, left eye blackened, the irises bloodshot, lip split and swollen. She moved slowly, wincing as she shrugged her way into her clothes.

"Sorry, we're late. We had to make a stop that took longer than expected. Ready to spend a night with the girls?" Becca asked.

"I think you should just move in with me indefinitely," I added.

"I - I don't think Manny would ..."

"Fuck that asshole! Why do you even care what he thinks after what he did to you?" Becca said.

"He'll come looking for me."

"And I'll kick his ass if he does," I said.

"Let's talk about all of this later. Right now, we need to get some wine, some ice cream, and some chocolate. I'll even watch a romantic comedy with you bitches. Everybody okay with that?" Becca said.

Trish smiled. I smiled too.

"Yeah. That sounds good," I said.

"Okay. I'm down too. You're right. Fuck Manuel," Trish answered.

Trish straightened her shirt and pants, then tried to apply some lipstick to her bruised lips.

"Ow! Fuck!"

"Don't worry about makeup. You don't need it. You know you always look good. I'm sure all the doctors and half the nurses in the place already want to fuck you. They're going to be sad to see you leave."

Trish sighed, looking in the mirror at her brutalized face. Her lip quivered and a tear raced down her cheek.

"Just get me the fuck out of here."

10

BECCA AND I WERE AT THE GYM, TRAINING TOGETHER FOR THE very first time. We left Trish at my apartment, sleeping off a night of wine, wine, ice cream, and wine, and healing from her bruises. We hadn't told her what we did to Manuel yet. All we told her was that we had "taken care of it." She didn't ask further, which was probably for the best. As much as she had to know he needed his ass kicked, she wouldn't be happy about us beating, humiliating, and emasculating him. We took her cellphone when we left, so she wouldn't be tempted to call him. That wouldn't be good.

The gym was empty. David Blanchard, the owner, had given me a key in exchange for a promise to sweep and mop the floors before classes began that afternoon. We stood inside the cage, facing each other. I was at least a head taller than her and fifty pounds heavier. Even knowing that she'd grown up doing martial arts (her father was a former pro-boxer and kickboxer, and she had two brothers who were amateur boxers), it was hard to believe this tiny little woman could teach me anything.

"Okay, so the first thing you need to do is get better at

slipping punches. These guys are going to be bigger and stronger than you. That strength advantage means they can make a lot of mistakes and still win. They only need to be perfect once. They'll always have a puncher's chance to end the fight with one wild, lucky shot. You understand?"

I nodded. I knew Becca was only trying to prepare me for what was coming, but it felt more like she was once again trying to talk me out of it.

"You want to slip outside the punches so you can counter safely. Always stay in countering range. You don't want to jump ten feet away to avoid a punch or kick. It wastes energy, and it keeps you on the defense. You want *him* on the defense. Like this, throw your jab."

I flicked out a jab, and Becca slipped to her right, avoiding my punch and exposing the left side of my face, ribs, and lead leg. She quickly popped me with a right cross, then threw a double kick to my rib and thigh.

"Shit!"

"I didn't hurt you. That was about fifty percent."

I rubbed my jaw, exaggerating my distress.

"If you can't take that little love tap, you're in trouble."

"I'm good. You just caught me off guard. But that was good stuff."

"Most people throw punches and kicks in a predictable pattern. Right, left, right, left. So, if a guy throws a jab, just go ahead and start slipping the straight right because nine out of ten times, that's what's coming next. If he throws a right first, then you prepare for that left hook. If you know what he's going to throw, it's easy to block, parry, or slip, and then to counter. The more often you counter punch, the more hesitant your opponent will be to throw. The less punches or kicks he throws, the easier it is to avoid those punches. If a guy throws a five punch combination, you're probably going to get hit with two or three of those shots unless he totally sucks, but if he only throws one or two shots at a time, you might be able to slip every one of them. So, what you want to do is interrupt his combinations with counters to keep him from putting together five and six punches in a row. Throw while he's throwing."

"But doesn't that mean I'll get hit?"

Becca smiled.

"You're going to get hit. This isn't one of those old Shaw Brothers kung fu flicks where guys are able to block every shot that's thrown at them. You have to bring ass to get ass. You don't want to get hit, don't get in the fight. All your defense will do is minimize the number of times you get hit."

I shook my head.

"But you said I shouldn't let these big guys hit me because they can end the fight with one punch?"

Becca shrugged.

"Well, that's the risk isn't it? You sure you want to do this?"

"We already placed the ad. I've already got responses from almost two dozen guys. Mostly assholes and weirdos, but eleven of them actually signed up to fight. I'm doing it."

Becca frowned and let out a long sigh, rolling her eyes and looking down at the floor.

"Then let me show you a few of my tricks. Throw your jab again."

I threw my jab, and Becca threw a leg kick, catching me on the thigh.

"Now, throw the jab again and try to block the kick."

I threw the jab again, and again, Becca tagged me on the thigh with a kick.

"Fuck! That hurt!"

"Toughen up, buttercup. Do you know why you keep getting kicked?"

I rubbed my legs, grimacing.

"Why?"

"Because when you throw a punch, when anyone throws a punch, they shift all of their weight to their front leg. It's impossible to punch and raise your leg to check a leg kick at the same time. Now, what else is open when you throw a jab?"

I remembered the shot to my jaw and my ribs.

"My ribs and my face."

Becca smiled, showing real enthusiasm. She was actually a pretty damn good teacher. I was learning more in one session with her than I had in almost a year of training at the gym.

"That's right! You can't throw a punch with your left hand and block the left side of your body at the same time. Every time someone throws a punch, they are exposing themselves to punishment. Your job is to make them pay. Make them miss, and make them pay. Okay, now let's work on a few more techniques."

We trained for two hours, only stopping between rounds for one-minute water breaks. When the training session ended, I was bruised and exhausted, but I felt like I was ready to kick some ass.

"Thanks, Becca. I never knew how good you were at this."

"Maybe I should enter the competition too?"

Becca smiled mischievously and winked at me. I smiled and quickly changed the subject.

"Do you have any clients today? I need to take a quick shower and head into the salon. I've got Marie Claire at noon."

Fight For Me 63

Becca nodded. The look on her face betrayed her disappointment. It wasn't like I'd never been with a woman before. I'd been with one or two over the years, but Becca and I had never gone down that road. Frankly, I saw how she treated her sexual conquests, and I did not want to wind up another notch in her dildo. Our friendship meant too much to me to sacrifice it for an orgasm, even multiple orgasms.

"Well, I hope you took tonight off. The first round of fights are tonight, right?"

My smile widened. I nodded enthusiastically.

"Fuck, yeah! I can't wait. It's going to be a twelve man tournament, single elimination."

"You said there were only eleven guys? Does that mean someone gets a free pass to the semi-finals?"

I laughed.

"Semi-finals? That makes it sound so -- I don't know -- official. But, no. I forgot there was another guy who signed up late last night to make it an even dozen."

"Well, make sure you get some rest before tonight."

"I'm not fighting anyone tonight. They're just fighting each other."

"Well, you never know how these things are going to go. I used to do tournaments. They rarely go as expected. People drop out at the last minute, get injured and can't continue. Soon, your twelve man tournament turns into a four man sparring session. Then, you might wind up fighting one of these guys sooner than you expected."

"Uh ... well ... shit. I hadn't thought of that. Do you think I'm ready?"

Becca frowned.

"Well, no. I don't think you're ready for any of this shit. Not emotionally anyway. I don't think you have any idea what you might be getting yourself into. I have no idea what you're getting yourself into. Not that you'd listen to me. But, physically, I think you'll be fine."

I hugged her.

"I love you, Becca. Thanks for being there for me. I feel a lot better with you helping me out. You're a real friend."

Becca pushed me away, holding me by the shoulders at arm's length. She shook her head. There was worry in her eyes along with what appeared to be annoyance.

"A real friend would be doing a better job of talking you out of this. I feel like I'm enabling you, but I know you are going to do this no matter what. The least I can do is make sure you're safe. And you know I love you too. Always have."

Uncharacteristically, Becca's voice was heavy with emotion. Something had changed between us, and I didn't know what or why. Was she just afraid of what I was doing, or that I wasn't doing it with her? Becca had never expressed any romantic interest before. We had always been like sisters. Maybe it was the idea of me actually meeting the man of my dreams, the prospect of losing me for good, that was fueling this new interest. My marriage to Steve hadn't been a threat because, as she told me once my marriage finally whimpered and died, she had never believed that relationship was going to work anyway. She knew the type of man I dreamed about, and Steve may have fit the type physically, but he was far from it mentally. He was just too weak. But this tournament presented an entirely different opportunity, a new, unknown threat. What I felt coming off of her in waves was her fear of losing me forever. And suddenly, I was afraid too.

11

WE HAD RENTED THE VERY SAME MMA GYM WHERE IT ALL started. Monster Maker's MMA. Predictably, Dillon showed up for the tournament. I felt bad, remembering how his bout with Armando had ended. But I couldn't help but be flattered that he was willing to try again to win me in battle. And, I had to admit, I felt safer knowing he was there in case things did get out of hand. Becca had impressed me with her abilities, but she was still a small woman.

"Hi, Dillon."

Dillon nodded at me stoically. He had his game face on. A moist heat spread in my panties and dripped down my thighs. *Oh God, this is going to be hot.*

The other men began to trickle in. Some were extremely handsome. Young, athletic, with finely-chiseled bodies and square jaws. Beautiful specimens of manhood. Others were monsters with hard, battle-scarred faces. Brutal men with broken noses, cauliflower ears, and massive muscular bodies built for destruction not beauty. The thought of ending up with one of them shook me to my core, but also excited me. The pretty boys were certainly attractive, but I'd tried pretty before with Steve, and it hadn't worked out so well. I wanted a man who scared me a little, and these other men were nothing if not scary.

The first fight was a glorified sparring match with two huge guys circling each other and throwing jabs and leg-kicks. One was a light-skinned black guy with a shaved head and a lazy eye. The other was a white guy with a crooked nose, an earlobe that looked like a piece of chewed up bubble gum, and long black hair pulled into a ponytail. Ponytail popped a jab that caught Lazy-Eye on the temple and jolted his head back. He followed it with a straight right to the belly and another jab, then a leg kick. That woke up Lazy-Eye. He charged, throwing a volley of wild hooks. One of the punches caught Ponytail flush on the jaw and wobbled him. That's when Ponytail shot in for a take down

Ponytail caught Lazy-Eye in a deep double-leg take down, tackling him off his feet. He lifted Lazy-Eye high in the air and slammed him hard to the canvas. The back of Lazy-Eye's head smacked the canvas, dazing him momentarily. Long enough for Ponytail to mount him and begin raining down punches, hammer-fists, and elbow strikes, desperate to end the fight.

Several punches landed flush as Lazy-Eye covered up and tried to squirm out from under him. A slashing downward elbow split Lazy-Eye's forehead open. Immediately, blood poured from the wound. Each subsequent strike splashed both combatants with blood until the battle became a gore-soaked spectacle as the two fighters continued to struggle against one another decorated in a fine sheen of liquid red.

Lazy-Eye managed to get his arms around Ponytail's

Fight For Me 67

torso and pull him tight against him. Then he used his legs to pull Ponytail's left leg into half guard. Before Ponytail could react, Lazy-Eye got his other leg free and was able to wrap both of his legs around Ponytail's waist, establishing full guard. He immediately began swinging his right leg up on to Ponytail's shoulders, trying for a triangle choke. With one hand gripping Ponytail's wrist, Lazy-Eye managed to get his leg up on to Ponytail's shoulders and to seize his own ankle, preventing his opponent from wriggling free. He then draped his other leg across his ankle, locking in the choke. He pulled the back of Ponytail's head down while still holding onto the man's wrist in a combination of an arm bar and a choke. Ponytail tapped out.

Lazy-Eye stood and raised his arms, leering at me through a veil of blood. I felt a chill race through me. Despite his drooping eyelid, he wasn't completely unattractive. Like most of the guys who'd shown up, he did have a remarkable physique. His face, however, was no prize.

Before exiting the cage, Lazy-Eye pointed to me and made a thrusting motion, then stuck out his tongue and licked his lips. It was crude, obscene, juvenile, and immediately left me rooting for his destruction. I was also not totally impressed with his fighting skills. He'd gotten lucky on the ground, but he'd been getting his ass-kicked. Luckily, I was pretty sure I could take him.

Becca was kind enough to mop the blood from the canvas before the next bout. It was Dillon vs a short, fireplug of a guy named Swayze who looked like he'd stepped right off the stage of a bodybuilding competition, bleached blond hair, spray tan, and all. I wondered how he could even move with all of that extra, unnecessary, muscle. Dillon put him through a clinic, easily avoiding Swayze's awkward take down attempts and punishing him with leg kicks, jabs, straight rights, and the occasional body kick. The fight went a full ten minutes with Swayze lumbering around eating shots and occasionally trying for a take down. Every so often, he would throw a wild looping hook that whizzed by a foot from its intended target. He was apparently a wrestler with little or no striking skills. Soon, both of his eyes were swollen almost shut and his face was bruised, swollen, and bleeding from his mouth, nose, and cuts above both eyes. He was breathing heavily and appeared on the verge of passing out from exhaustion when Dillon mercifully dispatched him with a head kick. Dillon nodded to me as he exited the cage.

"Let me guess, that's THE Dillon? The one that started all of this by almost choking you out?" Becca's asked. She was seated beside me, the only other non-combatant in the room.

"Yeah. I can't believe he came."

"He's not as short as you made him sound."

"That's because he's taller than you."

"I'm pretty sure I could still kick his ass. I mean, if I was in shape," Becca said.

The front door opened. I was positive that I had locked it before the tournament began. I stood up and rushed over to the door.

"Hey! Gym's closed!"

David Blanchard, the gym owner, walked in. I stopped, frozen in my tracks.

"Uh, hey David. I – uh, I thought you said I could have the gym to myself. I mean -- privately."

David nodded. He was dressed in black MMA shorts and a long-sleeved black rash guard. With his big red beard and burly, lumberjack build, he looked more like he was on

Fight For Me 69

his way to chop down a redwood than to train. I can't recall ever actually seeing him workout. He taught a class every so often, but mostly he was always in his office, paying bills, sending out invoices, signing up new members, and whatever else it took to keep the gym afloat, including renting it for a few hours to a crazy woman desperate to live out her fantasy.

"I heard you were holding some kind of a tournament. Thought it might be a perfect opportunity to come out of retirement. Give it one last go. You know what I mean?"

David had been a regular competitor on the Jiu Jitsu circuit. He even competed in the world championships in Brazil and Japan. But that had been a while ago. He'd been riding a desk for years, as far I knew, and he'd never competed in a full MMA match. The guys who'd shown up to fight for me were all killers.

"Yeah -- uh -- it's not really -- uh -- I mean -- it's not the kind of tournament you'd be interested in."

"An old dude? What is this, a geriatric competition?" Lazy-Eye asked.

David scoffed.

"How about I fight this joker first?"

The two fighters eyed each other menacingly. You could feel the testosterone like an aura of invisible pheromones wafting from them. I just couldn't understand how any woman would not have found it arousing. But ... this was David ... my coach. I couldn't let him fight for me -- could I?

"I -- I don't think you understand, David. This is ..." I didn't know what to say. Tell him the truth? That I was offering myself as a sex slave to whichever neanderthal emerged the victor in a gladiatorial game of "King Of The Mountain?"

He waved me off.

"I know exactly what it is. I saw the ad."

I was speechless. I had no idea David thought of me that way. He was my coach. Then again, so was Dillon. And if there was one thing I'd learned about men long ago, it was that men would do anything for pussy.

"So," David said, unzipping his gym bag and pulling out his mouthpiece and hand wraps. "Am I allowed to compete in my own gym or not?"

"Uh ... okay. Sure. Why not?"

Becca looked at me like I had lost my mind.

"You can't be serious?" she said, gesturing toward David with a sideways glance and a nod of the head, as if I had forgotten who we were discussing and just reminding me would end the argument.

"I'm looking for an alpha male. David qualifies."

"Yeah, but ... he's old."

I shrugged.

"If he can still fight, he can still fuck."

Becca shook her head.

"You have truly lost your fucking mind."

"So, I'm in?" David asked, already wrapping his hands.

"Yep. You're in."

"Good. Then who do I fight first?"

Becca spoke up. "Well, your friend over there has already fought. These are just the preliminary bouts. This is a single-elimination tournament. If you win your first bout, you move on to the quarter-final round. You might get a chance to fight him then. Right now ..."

I checked the list. There were still eight fighters who hadn't competed yet. I picked the first name I saw. "You can fight Jeremy."

I was hoping to find him someone easy. I had never met

Fight For Me 71

a badass named Jeremy. Jeremy was the name of the guy who delivered your newspaper, the kid who bagged your groceries at the local market, the altar boy at your church, the friend you've had since college who's never once tried to fuck you. A hulking guy with dark skin, almond eyes, a red Mohawk, a giant tattoo of an American eagle on his chest, and a tattoo of a wolf that covered his entire back, stood up and walked toward the cage. Or, it could be the name of a big, muscular, six-foot Native American warrior. *Sorry, David.*

The fight was swift and decisive. They walked into the cage. Becca locked the cage door behind them. She rang the bell, then they met in the center of the cage and touched gloves. David shot in for a double-leg take down immediately. He caught Jeremy just above the knees, draped him over his shoulders, lifted him off the ground, and slammed the big Native American hard to the canvas. He then secured the mount and transitioned from the mount into an arm-bar. Jeremy never tapped, never cried out in pain. He just allowed his arm to be broken. The sound of tendons snapping echoed like a gunshot through the gym.

"Oh, shit!" Becca cried out, leaping to her feet and running over to the cage to unlock it.

"God damn," I sighed. "That was -- that was amazing!"

"I didn't tap! The fight isn't over! I didn't tap!" Jeremy cried out.

"Your fucking arm is broken!" Becca said.

"It doesn't matter. I can still fight!"

"Not here you can't," David said. "I own this gym, and I'm telling you to get the fuck out and get your ass to the hospital."

The two men stood, staring each other down for a long

moment. I could tell the exact moment when the adrenaline left him and the pain hit. Jeremy's stoic mask cracked into a thousand shards. He grimaced in pain, cradling his arm as he quickly raced out of the cage and out the front door, pausing only to snatch up his keys.

"Okay, who's next?" David asked.

"Slow down, champ. We're not finished with the first round yet. We've got a few more fights to go."

David winked at me as he walked out of the cage and took his seat among the other fighters to watch the next contest.

The next fighter was a tall, awkwardly built, incongruous combination of muscle and fat, who looked more like a basketball player from somewhere in Eastern Europe than a fighter. He had to be nearly 7 feet tall. He stomped into the cage in giant, exaggerated, Fe Fi Fo Fum, motions then stood in the center with his head tilted up, chin held high, an arrogant, over-confident smirk on his face as he awaited the entrance of his opponent. The fighters had all picked their own opponents, drawing straws, flipping coins, arguing, and negotiating until they'd worked out the brackets. None of it mattered to me. I was only interested in the outcome.

The basketball player's opponent stood up and walked over to the cage. He was wearing a dark suit and had long dreadlocks all the way down his back that were speckled with flecks of gray, as was his goatee. His skin was glistening onyx, but his eyes were green and hazel. He had high cheekbones, a square jaw, and full, sensuous lips. He was beautiful in an exotic, non-traditional way. When he stepped up to the cage, he was still wearing a black, pin-striped suit with a solid black tie and a crisp white shirt. He stopped outside the cage, stooped to take off his shoes and socks,

Fight For Me

73

removed his suit jacket, and draped it over a nearby folding chair. He then loosened his tie, rolled up his sleeves, and stepped into the cage. The tall guy laughed in an exaggerated manner.

"You have got to be kidding me. Come on, pops. Just give up now before you get hurt. You ain't ready for this," the tall guy said.

The guy with the dreadlocks and cold green eyes smiled and walked to the center of the ring. He was not a small man, himself. He had to be nearly six-four and had large muscles bulging beneath his crisp white shirt. He looked strong, hard, every muscle there for a purpose rather than for aesthetics. Becca walked over to the cage and shut the door, locking the two fighters in.

"You have a big mouth, boy. Let's see if you can back it up," the guy with the dreadlocks said.

The two fighters stood toe to toe, face to face, staring each other down.

"What are you, like forty? Fifty?" The tall guy asked.

"Forty-five."

"I hope you know what you're doing."

Becca walked over to me before ringing the bell and whispered in my ear.

"Athena, this is crazy. That guy is going to fight wearing a shirt and tie? And he's got to be like twenty years older and six inches shorter than that tall dude. I mean, we don't have any emergency medical staff on hand if he gets hurt."

I nodded, barely listening.

"Did you see his eyes? They were beautiful. I don't think I've ever seen anyone with green eyes and skin that dark. He's fucking gorgeous."

"You aren't listening."

"I'm listening. Just ring the bell."

Becca shook her head.

"This is getting out of hand."

"Fine, I'll ring it," I said.

I stood up and walked over to the round timer beside the cage. The fighters separated, retreating to opposite sides of the ring. I rang the bell -- and all hell broke loose.

12

THE TALL GUY THREW A HEAD KICK. THE BIG GUY WITH THE green eyes and dreadlocks leaned back and the kick sailed harmlessly over his head. Before the tall guy could plant his foot back on the floor, Green Eyes stepped forward at a forty-five-degree angle and kicked his supporting leg out from under him. The tall guy almost did a somersault, flipping over backwards and landing hard, with his head, neck, and shoulders slamming into the mat. Green Eyes followed by kicking the tall guy in the jaw, then stomping him in the face until he ceased all movement. Everyone in the room fell silent. I didn't know what to say. I was in shock.

"So, I would like to propose new rules. I'm going to stand here in this cage, and I will fight each of you, one by one, until there are none of you left."

"Man, you're fucking crazy!" said the guy with the lazy eye who'd won the earlier fight. I looked over at Dillon, who looked at me and shrugged.

"If I'm crazy, perhaps you should try me," Green Eyes said. Lazy Eye stood.

Green Eyes was still standing in the center of the cage, refusing to give it up.

"Wait a minute!" I said, leaping to my feet, standing there defiantly, one hand on my hip, the other waving a finger in the air. "That isn't how this works."

Green Eyes turned toward me. Even with a hundred feet and a cage between us, I could feel the power of his gaze as his eyes met mine.

"It's how it works now. If anyone disagrees, let him step up first," Green Eyes said.

"And who are you?"

He smiled.

"Tyrell. But you may call me Master."

I shook my head.

"Not yet, I won't"

"Soon," Tyrell replied confidently.

"Well, fuck you Tyrell! You can't just come in here takin' over shit!" the guy with the lazy eye said.

Tyrell gestured him forward.

"Then come in here and convince me of the error of my ways."

Lazy- Eye rushed into the cage.

They didn't wait for the bell to ring or the cage door to shut. Lazy-Eye charged forward and threw a big overhand right hook that Tyrell slipped under and answered with a left hook to Lazy-Eye's ribcage, an uppercut to the solar plexus that doubled his opponent over. Tyrell then locked both arms on either side of his opponent's neck, cupping the back of Lazy-Eye's head in his massive hands, then jerked his opponent's head down into his knee, one, two, three, four times in rapid succession. Tyrell caught him as Lazy-Eye went limp in his arms. He carried his fallen opponent over to the cage door and tossed him out. Lazy-Eye landed

Fight For Me

face-first on the wrestling mats that surrounded the cage and lay still, a small puddle of blood forming on the mat around his head. Were it not for his loud, sonorous breathing, I would have thought he was dead.

"Next opponent," Tyrell said.

A short, stocky, bald black guy with muscles like boulders rushed into the cage. He looked like the stereotypical wrestler. He shot in for a take down, got caught with a knee to the chin, and finished off with a guillotine. The wrestler tried to tap, but Tyrell didn't let him go until he was completely unconscious.

"Okay, come on. Let's get this over with. Who's going to be next?"

A guy with platinum blond hair shaved into a military-style crew cut and tattoos covering every visible inch of his body from his neck to his ankles stepped forward. He was about six-one with a lean, athletic build. Barely two hundred pounds. He tried to stand with Tyrell, throwing flashy, spinning kicks that Tyrell easily blocked before trapping him against the cage and hammering him to sleep with elbows that made a bloody ruin of the guy's once handsome face. Tyrell dragged him across the cage by his ankle and tossed him out of the cage as well.

Three fighters stood up and walked out the door. Obviously, Tyrell was more than they were prepared for.

"Okay, I'm next," Dillon said.

He walked past me on his way to the cage.

"You don't have to do this, Dillon," I said.

He smiled. His eyes looked sad. He knew he was going to lose.

"You know I do."

"This guy is dangerous. You saw what he did to those other fighters."

"He's standing in the way of me getting to you. I've lost before."

I tried my best smile, but it faltered. As much as I was enjoying the fights, flattered beyond words that they had all come to fight for me, I didn't want to see Dillon hurt.

"Please, be careful."

He smiled that same sad smile, then walked into the cage. And never walked out.

The fight was brutal. He lasted longer than all the others who fought Tyrell that night. He landed a couple punches, two jabs and a straight right that opened a cut on Tyrell's upper lip. Dillon had the speed advantage, but experience was definitely on the side of Tyrell. It was almost as if he could anticipate what Dillon was going to throw. I remembered what Becca had told me about how most people throw strikes in predictable patterns, right followed by a left, left followed by a right. She'd said that once you had their rhythm, knew what they were going to throw, you'd know where they were vulnerable to counter strikes. Tyrell's confidence was an obvious result of having been through many wars. He'd seen it all before. Nothing Dillon threw was a surprise.

Dillon landed a few leg kicks, and a spinning back kick to Tyrell's body. But Tyrell caught his leg, wrapped his arm around Dillon's shin, and tucked it under his arm ... and smiled. All the color drained from Dillon's face. He knew what was about to happen. Becca squeezed my thigh.

"No."

"What?" I asked.

Becca was already running toward the cage.

Still holding onto Dillon's leg with his left, Tyrell brought his right elbow down on Dillon's knee, driving it straight through the patella with a wet ripping sound followed by a pop as tendons tore and snapped. Dillon screamed. Tyrell let go of Dillon's leg and allowed him to fall to the floor. Becca opened the cage, and she and I ran inside and helped carry Dillon out as he moaned and cursed and writhed in agony.

"Take him to the hospital for me, Becca. Please?"

"And what are you going to do? You have to end this. It's gotten way out of control. That guy's a fucking lunatic! He broke Dillon's leg on purpose!" Becca said, pointing at Tyrell, who remained standing in the center of the cage.

"I've got David here with me."

"I won't let anything happen to her. I promise. I'll handle it. Please, just take Dillon to the hospital. He looks like he's going to pass out."

"I'm not going to pass out. I'll be fine," Dillon said.

"You don't look fine."

Becca helped support Dillon, wrapping an arm around his waist while he draped an arm over her shoulder.

"Be careful, David," Dillon said. "That guy is ... he's not like normal fighters. Look at him. He's not even sweating."

David, Dillon, Becca, and I all turned to look at Tyrell, who still stood in the center of the cage in dress pants and a dress shirt, rolling up his sleeves. The shirt was completely dry except for a few flecks of blood from the cut Dillon had opened on his lip. That was the only indication he'd been in a fight at all. His cold, green eyes regarded us all dispassionately. Like we were specimens in a petri dish.

"Don't fight him, David. There's something not right about him." Dillon winced and grimaced, biting his lip against the pain. "Fuck! This hurts! Let's get out of here. I need some fucking painkillers."

"Okay, I've got you," Becca said.

"Just get me to the car. I can drive myself. You stay here with Athena."

"Are you sure?"

"I'm sure I don't want to leave her alone with that psycho. Besides, I only need one leg to drive."

Dillon hopped out the door and into the parking lot, supporting himself on his uninjured leg and using Becca as a crutch. After tucking him into the car, Becca hurried back into the gym.

David turned toward me. His face was a rictus of anger.

"You need to call this shit off! I'm not going to have people getting hurt in my gym!"

"That was fucked up, but people get hurt in here all the time. What is it you always say? 'We ain't baking cookies in here.' If it ends now, he's the winner. You're the only fighter left. All the rest quit or he's already beaten them."

David looked up into the cage. It was obvious he didn't want this guy to win. He was pissed off about what Tyrell had done to Dillon's leg. But, it was equally obvious that he was afraid. Finally, anger won out, and David stepped into the cage. I locked the door behind them and rang the bell.

13

David wouldn't quit. The first leg kick Tyrell landed buckled David's leg and brought him to his knees. It was followed by a head kick that I thought would decapitate him. Tyrell's shin connected with David's forehead and sent him crashing to the canvas, face first. Tyrell smiled at me and prepared to exit the cage to claim his prize when David staggered to his feet. His eyes were glazed, and he looked unsteady, but then they suddenly cleared, and he charged.

The miraculous recovery and surprising burst of aggression startled Tyrell. David managed to catch one of his legs, trying for a single-leg take down. Tyrell pushed down on David's head, hopping on one foot as he tried to pull his leg out of David's grasp, but David was tenacious. For a moment, I thought he would get the take down. I was curious to see how Tyrell would do on his back. No one had managed to take him off his feet so far. But then, still hopping on one leg, his other leg trapped in David's arms, he jumped up and landed a knee to David's jaw that sent him falling over backwards. David rolled and leaped back to his feet, staggering and shaking his head to clear the haziness. Just like before, in seconds, his eyes were clear, and he was ready to fight again. I jumped to my feet and cheered. He wasn't winning, but he wasn't going down easy.

"Go, David! You can get him!"

Becca grabbed my arm and spun me around to face her.

"Stop this! He's going to get killed in there!"

I looked at Becca and shook my head.

"Hell no! They're both men. This is what men do. They fight. No one is forcing either of them to do this. They know what they're doing."

Becca looked shocked.

"Are you fucking kidding me? Do you even hear yourself? I - I don't even know who you are anymore!"

Becca was furious. She glared at me, a tempest raging behind her eyes. For a moment I thought she was about to hit me. Her fists were balled, and she was breathing heavily. Her brow was furrowed, and a vein in her temple stood out prominently. I stood up close to her so that I towered above her. If she was going to hit me, dammit, she was going to get hit back.

"No. You *don't* know who I am anymore."

Becca's face relaxed. A calm acceptance seeped into her features, and she just looked sad, weary, disappointed. It was heartbreaking to see. Becca was my oldest friend, and I was selling her out for a man, for men. No, I was selling her out for a fetish, my fetish for violence. For violent men. Becca shook her head. Tears leaked from her eyes, and she quickly wiped them away.

"I'm done. You're on your own. I can't be a part of this -- whatever the fuck this is. I hope you know what you're doing."

With that, she turned her back on me and walked away.

"I hope I do too," I said as I watched the gym door close behind her.

When I turned around, David was making a desperate rush at the big, dark-skinned fighter with the dreadlocks and the soulless green eyes. He swung a volley of short, tight hooks, uppercuts, and overhand rights, varying his attack to the body and head in an attempt to confuse his opponent. Tyrell seemed to see every blow coming, until David threw a right hook to the body followed by an overhand right, breaking the predictable left-right-left-right pattern. The overhand right caught Tyrell flush on the jaw and drove him back to the cage, where David managed to land a left hook to the body and a left uppercut that knocked Tyrell's head back. I stood up and clapped, exhilarated by David's unexpected success.

"Yeah! Kick his ass!"

But then it was over. Tyrell landed a knee to David's solar plexus just as David was rushing in to finish him off. I could hear the air woosh from David's lungs. It looked like Tyrell's knee was about to bust through David's back. Tyrell threw another flying knee that crashed into David's jaw, and I watched in stunned, horrified amazement as my former coach wilted to the canvas. Tyrell mounted him and began raining down punches and elbows on David's unprotected face. David's skin cut, then his skull cracked, then shattered, then completely came apart. Blood and brains exploded across the floor in a gruesome Rorschach. I screamed and kept screaming as I watched Tyrell rise from the blood-soaked canvas, his knuckles and his previously crisp white shirt dripping red.

"Come here," he growled, pointing at his feet.

I considered leaving, just walking away and calling the police. Tyrell had just murdered my coach, the guy who'd trained me for the last year. But then I remembered. He murdered him for me. And something about that thought made me feel just as guilty, complicit in the act. It also made me feel other things that I didn't want to think about, didn't want to admit to, but that moved me, nonetheless, to walk to the cage door, unlock it, and kneel at Tyrell's feet.

14

———

"You are mine now. Say it," Tyrell said, gripping the back of my head in one of his large, spider-like hands.

His fingers were like iron talons, digging into my scalp. He twisted my hair in his hand as he balled it into a fist, jerking my head back and forcing me to look up at him, to meet his steely, soulless gaze. There was nothing in those eyes that could be reasoned with. No compassion. No humanity. It was like being eye-to-eye with another species, one that had supplanted humans as the apex predator.

"Say it!"

I trembled. The deep resonant reverberation of his voice was like a subwoofer with the bass turned all the way up to a window-rattling, earthquake, fuck-the-neighbors, rumble, pounding against my chest, vibrating through my bones. His presence was overwhelming. I felt tiny for the first time I could remember.

"I'm yours."

"Of course you are."

He took out his cock. A long, thick, beautiful black cock like something from a porn movie. I opened my mouth reflexively, before he could tell me to, and Tyrell pulled my head forward, easing his full length between my lips, past my tonsils, and down my throat as I fought off my gag reflex. He rocked his hips forward and back, fucking my throat, gently at first, then more aggressively when he realized I could take it. As large as he was, he was neither the first man to fuck my throat nor the biggest. Though certainly one of the top three. I reached up and cupped his testicles in my hand, rubbing them softly.

A rumbling purr vibrated in Tyrell's chest as he neared orgasm. When he came, he filled my mouth with his seed, still pumping in and out of my mouth. Semen spilled out the sides of my mouth as I gagged and choked, dripping off my chin and down between my breasts.

When Tyrell released his grip on my head and withdrew his pulsating manhood from my throat, I gasped for air, coughing and retching, his seed still drooling from my open mouth along with my own saliva. I was aware of Tyrell looking down at me with mild amusement. I wanted to tell him to go fuck himself, but I was intrigued by the fact that he was showing any emotion at all. Apparently, killing a man didn't stir any emotions within him at all, but watching a woman nearly choke to death on his cock was pure comedy. I imagined I did look pretty comical though.

"Jesus Christ!" I said, still catching my breath.

Tyrell nodded then began taking off his belt. A thrill went through me, thinking he was about to fuck me right there in the cage, right beside David's corpse, in a pool of his blood. It was a terrible, ugly, morbid thought, but it aroused me nonetheless. And I felt terrible about it. The guilt somehow made the whole thing even more exciting, however. But Tyrell didn't want to fuck me. Instead, he pulled my pants down, pushed me up against the cage, and

Fight For Me 87

began spanking my ass and the back of my thighs with the belt.

"Please," I said, but I wasn't sure if I was begging him to stop or not to. I began to cry. First a few solitary tears, then a flood. I sobbed, letting out all the guilt I felt over David's death and my previous lack of remorse and perverse thoughts of fucking in his blood, how I had just sucked the cock of his murderer, how I had spoken to Becca, my best friend, dismissed her as if she meant nothing to me, and for what? I had betrayed her for sex with a psychopath. I wept also in fear of what this man would do to me next, whether he would kill me, torture me, and what I would do if he didn't, if he kept me alive to fulfill my promise to be his sex slave. The spanking continued until my entire world became pain. Until all the guilt and sorrow and fear was gone, and only the pain remained. It continued until I was drunk off the pain, until endorphins flooded my bloodstream and I felt like I was flying, until I wanted nothing more but for him to continue spanking me until I stopped crying.

When Tyrell released me, I collapsed to the cage floor, trembling from the adrenaline and dopamine coursing through my system like a shot of opioids. I watched as Tyrell threaded his belt back through the loops. He removed his blood-soaked shirt and the equally drenched tank top beneath it, draped the shirt over David's face to hide the gruesome destruction from sight, then tossed the tank top into the blood beside the body.

He walked out of the cage, stopped to put his socks and shoes on, then picked up a towel and wiped the blood from his chest, arms, stomach, and back. He then retrieved his suit jacket from the chair he'd draped it over and put it on over his bare torso.

I was still lying there in the cage, trembling, quivering on the floor like some frightened animal. I watched him take a cellphone from his pocket and make a phone call. Then he removed the sim card from the phone, crushed it in his hand, tossed it into a nearby wastebasket, then took a new sim card from his pocket and inserted it into his phone. He did it all automatically, reflexively, without thinking about it. Through the sluggish haze of endorphins, my mind slowly registered the fact that Tyrell had been prepared for this, that David's death had been no surprise to him. The entire time his eyes were on me, watching me. I got the impression he was trying to decide what to do with me, whether or not he should let me live. I had no strength to fight him. He had just dismantled the man who'd been training me for a year, and did so with relative ease. There was no hope of me fighting this man. Everything Becca had taught me would be useless against a beast like Tyrell. It would be like throwing pebbles at a tank.

It was a full hour before I heard a gentle knock on the door of the gym. During that time, I hadn't left the cage, and Tyrell hadn't re-entered it, leaving me alone with my fears and doubts, regret and remorse, while he made several other phone calls. Tyrell walked over and opened the door, still keeping his eye on me.

I still had not moved. I had stopped shivering. The numbness and euphoria the endorphins provided had passed, and now I felt only the pain of where Tyrell's belt had bruised and welted my skin. I had been too afraid to move, so I had just laid there in the cage, watching Tyrell watch me.

Three guys ranging in ages from early twenties to late forties and an older Mexican woman, who seemed to be in charge, walked through the door carrying mops and buckets

Fight For Me 89

and trash bags. One of the men carried a saw. Tyrell pointed them to the cage. The clean-up crew had arrived to clean the gym and dispose of David's body.

Tyrell finally walked back into the cage. I wanted to run from him, to fight him off. Instead, I just laid there, frozen, as he walked over to me, knelt down, and scooped me up in his arms, cradling me against his powerful chest like an infant.

I began to tremble again as he carried me out of the cage and out the front door of the gym. The last sight I saw was one of the Mexican guys sawing off David's arm. That wet, ripping sound will be with me forever. Tyrell kicked the door shut behind us as he walked me out across the parking lot to where a black sedan sat idling. The driver stepped out and opened the door for us. Tyrell laid me down gently on the back seat, then climbed in beside me.

"Home?" the driver asked.

Tyrell only nodded, then we were leaving the parking lot. Leaving the blood and carnage behind.

Who the fuck is this man? What have I gotten myself into?

15

I don't know what I was expecting, a mansion in some exclusive gated community, a chateau by the beach, maybe even a crack house in some inner-city slum, anything but a luxurious suite in a four star hotel in the middle of the financial district.

After dismissing our driver with a nod of the head and a few cryptic words— "Tell Byrd he did good. He's off the hook for now."—Tyrell led me through the suite to his bedroom, where an enormous jacuzzi tub dominated one entire wall, separating the bedroom from the bathroom. He turned on the tub as we passed it, then began peeling out of his clothes.

I stood in the center of this enormous room, hands clasped in front of me, nervously shifting from one foot to the other, uncertain what to do. I watched him, then blushed when I realized I was waiting for him to tell me what to do, waiting for his command. It was almost frightening how easily I slipped into this submissive mindset when confronted with a truly dominant man, and Tyrell was as dominant a man as ever walked this earth. He had proven himself the alpha male in combat. Now, I was waiting for him to do the same in the bedroom.

He hadn't removed his pants during his fights, or even when I'd sucked his cock. This would be my first look at his entire body. And It was magnificent.

His chest, shoulders, legs, and arms were armored in thick, striated muscle. Bulging veins roped their way from the back of his hands up his arms and across his chest, and up his calves to snake their way up his powerful thighs. His stomach was not a full six-pack, but it was obvious he worked at it. The top four abdominal muscles bulged through the skin like two rows of bricks, but the final two were obscured by a small layer of fat. It was hard to believe a man with the discipline to turn his body into a perfect weapon of destruction had any issues with diet. I doubted his body had ever seen a carbohydrate, at least not in many years. He was just older, as the streaks of white in his goatee and dreadlocks attested to. And with age came a slower metabolism that even a spartan diet and superhuman workout routine could only do so much to combat. And I had to admit, seeing even that one small bit of imperfection on a body so perfect made him even sexier, because it meant he was human. That he wasn't some new advancement in human evolution. Tyrell was just a man. Just a different type of man than I'd ever met before.

As I stood there, waiting for Tyrell to tell me what to do, watching as he filled the huge bathtub and turned on the jets, the reality of the situation I was in came crushing down upon me. I was alone in a hotel room with a man who could murder someone with his bare hands, then make the body disappear with a phone call.

"Who are you?" I whispered, barely loud enough for him to hear. I closed my eyes and silently hoped he hadn't heard me. I dreaded the answer to that question would make me even more of an accomplice than I already was.

There had been no way for me to know that Tyrell was going to kill David, that he was even capable of doing so. Even though the entire tournament had been my idea, and I could have stopped David from entering but didn't, I could find solace, claim innocence in my ignorance. I didn't know Tyrell was a psychopath. But now I did, and yet I'd left with him, come back to his hotel room, had his cock in my throat, and swallowed his seed. If I was ever questioned by the police, I would say I was scared, that I'd only gone with him out of fear for my life. I'd probably tell Becca the same thing. But Becca would know I was lying. I couldn't lie to her any more than I could lie to myself. And that's why I was afraid to learn any more about the man who now owned me. I was grateful when he ignored my question and continued to prepare our bath.

"Take off your clothes."

I froze at those words. All the insecurities I'd conquered in the gym this past year came bubbling to the surface. What would this man with the near perfect body, think of my wide hips, the fat on my thighs, the slight bulge of my stomach? Would he be disappointed in this body he had literally killed for? And what would he do to me if he wasn't pleased?

Tears rushed to my eyes. My hands trembled as they slowly moved to comply with my master's command. I didn't move fast enough, apparently. Tyrell strode over to me, grabbed me by the shirt with both of his massive hands, and tore it in half. When he grabbed for my sports bra, I stepped back away from him, raising my hand, palms out. A gentle barrier I knew he could walk through easily had he wanted to. He had already made it clear that he could take whatever he wanted from me, and I would have little choice.

"I've got it. I-I'll do it."

Tyrell stepped back, folded his arms across his chest, and waited, staring holes through me with a look of impatience and barely suppressed rage. Even the slightest vexation of his will seemed to anger him. Without saying a word, he had clearly communicated a dire warning to me:

"Be careful. You know what I am capable of."

And, of course, I knew exactly what he was capable of. I had seen him easily dismantle men bigger, stronger, and more skillful than me. What terrified me was that I had no idea how he'd done it. He was obviously big and strong, but some of the men had been bigger, and presumably stronger. He was older than they were, so I chalked it up to skill born of experience. But what experience? Where had he gained such a high level of experience? What fight league had he been part of? How many fights must he have had to allow him to exude such confidence and then back it up so expertly and emphatically?

As I stripped for him, finding myself aroused by the softening of his expression, the deep exhalation of breath as my sizable breasts flopped free from my sports bra, the undisguised lust in his eyes as his gaze roamed my curves, the question slipped out.

"Where did you fight?"

He ignored my question, still staring at my body as I wriggled out of my tights. So, I repeated it.

"Y- you're obviously pretty experienced. You - um - you don't learn to fight like, like *that* just sparring in the gym. You must have had some high level professional fights, right?"

I was completely naked now, standing there fully

Fight For Me

exposed in front of him, feeling unusually modest, trying to cover myself with my hands.

Tyrell reached out and roughly jerked my hands away.

"Don't. I want to see you."

Walking slowly around me at arm's length, Tyrell appraised his prize. A leering, malevolent smile pulled up the corners of his mouth. He looked like a mischievous child contemplating pulling the wings off a fly. A shiver went through me. Goosebumps raised all over me. The self-consciousness I'd felt earlier had now quintupled. I trembled, fighting back tears, mortified by the fear of being rejected by this beautiful, magnificent killer.

"S-so, where?"

"Where, what?" Tyrell growled in agitation, annoyed at having his creepy, lecherous contemplation of my body interrupted.

"Where did you fight?"

"Get in the tub," Tyrell said, ignoring my question once again. He turned and climbed into the enormous hot tub, giving me a look at his amazing body from a new angle and providing a momentary relief from his merciless gaze. I let out a sigh, then rushed over to the tub, eager to comply with his order, both to spare myself whatever consequences this violent man might deal out for non-compliance and because the hot tub would hide all the flaws I perceived in my own body.

The hot tub was hotter than I would have preferred, almost scalding. The welts and bruises on my ass and thighs from the beating Tyrell had given me sang out in agony as I eased down into the tub. I felt like my skin was melting off and wondered how Tyrell could stand it. But once I acclimated to it, it was soothing. I felt my muscles begin to relax and only then realized how tense they had been.

Tyrell gestured for me to move closer. I obeyed, sliding across the hot tub into his arms. Tyrell squirted a lavender and jasmine scented oil into his palms and began massaging my neck and shoulders. I closed my eyes and melted into him. He massaged my back, not gently. His strong fingers bored into the knotted muscles along my spine, suffocating the muscles until they collapsed and went completely limp. He massaged my hips and thighs. I saw his manhood stir beneath the water like some mysterious underwater creature breaking through a cloud of sea foam. He obviously held great appreciation for a woman with curves. This made me relax even more. His fingers kneaded my thighs and calves like dough. He massaged my arms, my feet, even my hands to the very tips of my fingers. I was so completely relaxed, I felt like I could fall asleep.

Abruptly, Tyrell pulled the plug to drain the tub, then stood and stepped out of the tub. He was fully erect, his turgid flesh pointing like a thick ebon spear as he walked across the bathroom to retrieve a towel. He gestured for me to stand, and I quickly complied, remembering to suppress the urge to cover my breasts and stomach, not wanting to anger this man who could be so gentle yet, in an instant, so brutal.

He dried me off, taking his time to wipe and pat away each and every drop of water. He then hung up the towel and walked back into the bedroom, gesturing for me to follow, which I, of course, did without hesitation. He turned out lights as he walked through the suite to the bed until only a small lamp by the king sized bed remained lit. Tyrell pulled back the covers and patted the mattress for me to lay down beside him. I was excited, yet terrified. This monstrous human being was about to fuck me? Rape me? Make love to me? I had no idea what to expect.

Fight For Me

97

I laid down, trembling all over as I stared up at his face, trying to read his thoughts through his stoic expression. He began to rub my arms, squeezing them gently, then my shoulders, then my breasts, my hips, my thighs. The lust in his eyes was something mad and furious. He knelt down and rubbed his cheek over the small mound of my belly, the little paunch I had been working my ass off to get rid of. He kissed it, then took a large chunk of it in his mouth, biting it softly. He repeated this same action against my hips, rubbing his face over them, sucking and biting them, then my thighs, then back to my belly, and up to my breasts. I continued to tremble, terrified each time he took a bite of my flesh, afraid he would rip a chunk out of me. But, also amazed by his gentleness, by the way he seemed almost entranced by my flesh, enraptured by every curve, great and small.

Tyrell kissed, sucked, bit, and caressed every inch of me until I was so wet, I was positive I had soaked completely through the mattress. Then, I felt his teeth bite my inner thigh. Hard. I yelped and struggled as he bit deep. I fought to free myself from his teeth, but he only bit deeper. I saw my own blood ooze out from the corners of his mouth, and panic gripped me. Finally, he released me. I looked down and saw his teeth marks welling with blood. He smiled at me through blood stained teeth, then dove back down, burying his face in my sex.

When I felt his mouth against my clitoris, I winced in anticipation of the pain, expecting to feel his teeth biting me again, biting me there. Instead, I felt the gentle flick of his tongue. Then his lips and tongue, sucking my clitoris, then my labia, then his tongue inside me, slippery and wet, fucking me with it. Then back to my clit, then his long, thick fingers inside me, one, two, then three as his tongue lashed my engorged clit. All of my fear of him was gone now, replaced by the most profound ecstasy. I came with a shout that startled me, my body convulsed, legs twitching and spasming as waves of pleasure buffeted me like gunfire. Tyrell slowed the movement of his tongue and his fingers, but never stopped. Soon, I was building to another thunderous orgasm.

"Oh, shit! Oh, fuck! Oh, God! Oh, Goddamn!"

Then, I came again, and again. Then I felt Tyrell's hand around my throat, then his other hand, the one that had been inside me, forcing its way into my mouth. Then Tyrell lifted his head from between my legs, staring down at me as he choked me and forced me to taste my own juices.

I felt him force his enormous cock inside me and begin to thrust urgently, while his grip on my throat tightened, slowly cutting off my oxygen while his thrusts became longer, deeper, harder, brutally battering my sex. I came again, hard, harder than ever before. Right before I lost consciousness.

When I awoke, I was lying on my back. Tyrell was curled up against me, one leg draped over both of mine, his shrinking cock pressed my hip, arms wrapped around my waist, his head on my breasts, sucking one of my nipples like an infant nursing, completely asleep. I looked down at him. His face looked peaceful, serene in a way I hadn't thought possible when I was watching him dismantle his opponents in the cage, or fuck me like he had paid for me while choking me unconscious.

My nipple felt sore, but I was afraid to move. I didn't want to disturb him. I was afraid of what he might do. And, I liked looking at him like this. He looked almost sweet, childlike and innocent despite the gray in his hair and the hard

Fight For Me

lines in his face. I watched him for what felt like an hour or longer before I finally fell asleep.

I woke the next day to room service wheeling in a breakfast banquet of eggs, scrambled, poached, over easy, sunny side up, Benedict, and several choices of omelets. Bacon, sausage, steak, pancakes, waffles, french toast, bagels, smoked salmon with cream cheese, tomatoes, and capers, and assorted fruits along with various muffins and danishes. There was a choice of milk, orange juice, apple juice, mimosas, a pitcher of bloody Mary, and a pot of coffee. Tyrell stood by the window in a black silk robe that he hadn't bothered to close, underneath which he was completely naked. He had showered, and his skin glistened with scented oils.

Tyrell's nudity didn't appear to bother the room service waiter, who went dutifully about the business of laying out the buffet, pouring the coffee, along with two glasses of mimosas and two bloody marys . When the waiter was finished, he smiled at me.

"I hope everything is to your liking, madame?"

I was still blinking the sleep from my eyes and trying to decipher dream from reality, slowly remembering where I was and the events that had led me here.

"It- it's fine. I mean, it's perfect. Thank you."

Tyrell stepped forward and handed the man a tip. A crisp hundred dollar bill. The waiter smiled, did a flamboyant little bow, then turned and walked out the door, closing it quietly behind him.

"I didn't know what you like to eat, so I had him bring a little of everything."

"I see that. Thank you. That was very sweet."

Tyrell winced at the compliment, as if he'd taken it as an insult. I tensed, afraid I'd done something wrong. Afraid he would punish me. His face softened again, and I let out a sigh.

"What would you like to drink?"

"The mimosas look good right now. Thanks."

Tyrell handed me a glass flute filled with champagne and orange juice, then grabbed a cup of coffee for himself.

"So, what do you do that you can afford to live like this? Are you some kind of businessman or a criminal?"

My mouth has never been well disciplined. As afraid as I was of this man, I was even more curious about him. I wanted to get to know him. I was doing what I would have done had this been a normal date, had we met on a dating website, or through mutual friends. I was sizing him up for a relationship. *Could I love someone who terrified me?* I wasn't certain. I could certainly fuck him. There was no questioning that. My fear of him was an aphrodisiac. For us both, I suspected.

"Is there really a difference?" Tyrell replied.

Tyrell smiled, and it was a beautiful smile, with none of the malice that had been in the expression the night before. He looked almost human now.

I smiled too. The expression was contagious.

"I take that to mean the latter. Drug dealer?"

"Killer," Tyrell answered, so nonchalantly I was certain I'd misheard him. He took a sip of coffee, eyes focused on mine, reading my expression.

"Did you say you were a killer?"

"You already knew that. I killed someone to win you."

"Yes ... but ..." I said. Not sure what I could add. He was right. He had killed David in front of me, then I had begged Tyrell to fuck me in my friend's blood right after sucking Tyrell's cock. I couldn't exactly pretend innocence or moral outrage now.

Fight For Me   101

"You kill people for money?"

"That's one of the reasons."

I knew I shouldn't ask, but curiosity has always been my weakness, and this dark and handsome mystery was too tempting to resist.

"What are the other reasons?"

Tyrell put his cup down after taking another sip, then walked over to me. He wrapped one of his massive hands around my throat, slowing squeezing, increasing the pressure as he studied my response. I didn't resist. There would have been no point to it. If Tyrell wanted me dead, then I would die, no matter how hard I fought. We both knew it, but it was clear that Tyrell wanted to emphasize it in that moment, to make it clear where our relationship stood. I would live and die according to his will. I was his slave. His plaything. His property. He leaned down so that his face was inches from mine.

"I kill because I enjoy it. It relaxes me."

It relaxes me

He'd said it so calmly. So passionlessly. Remorselessly. Murder made him feel better, and so he killed. It was as simple as that for him. Scratching an itch, indulging a craving. The way some people eat chocolate or ice cream, Tyrell took lives. Neither his voice nor his expression betrayed any feelings of guilt or shame over this. If he had any misgivings at all regarding this peculiar form of therapy, he hid them deep within. So deep, he was utterly unaware of them.

"I want to watch."

"What?"

The words slipped out of my mouth the moment the thought entered my head. All of my filters seemed to have been dashed away along with my freedom. If I had taken a moment to really think about it, I would have perhaps reconsidered my request. This was taking me into even darker territory. But I had already left the light far behind the moment I put together that tournament and offered myself as a living trophy. I had embraced the darkness, fucked it, sucked its cock, swallowed its seed, become its slave.

"I want to watch you do what you do. I want to see you murder someone."

A sardonic grin broke across his face. It looked incongruously jovial on such a hard and brutal visage.

"You already have."

I should have left it alone. He had just given me a way out, an opportunity to retract my errant question. But, as I said, I hadn't been making very rational decisions.

"No. That was someone who angered you. He hit you, and you lost your temper. I want to see what it looks like when you deliberately plan to kill someone."

Tyrell shook his head.

"No. You don't."

"I do. I want you to show me how to get away with murder."

Tyrell raised an eyebrow.

"Why?"

I thought about Manuel. That moment when I had him down, had his back, choking him, feeling his breathing slow. The only thing that had prevented me from holding that choke until his last breath had been the certainty of getting caught, going to prison for the rest of my life. If I thought I could have gotten away with it, Manuel would no longer exist.

"Because some people deserve to die," I said.

Tyrell studied my eyes, looking for the truth in them, or the lie. That bemused expression was still on his face. He

Fight For Me 103

regarded me the way one might regard a roaring lion cub who could do no more than snarl and squeak, as threatening as a house cat.

"I could show you, but then I would have to kill you. I don't leave witnesses."

There was no smile on his face this time. I felt a chill race the length of my vertebrae, raising goosebumps.

I don't leave witnesses.

But, I had already seen him kill once. Did that mean he was already planning to end my life once he'd finished using my body? I looked him in the eyes, hoping to see something in them to assuage my fears. Something to tell me that he wouldn't hurt me. But I knew he would. I knew he was not only fully capable of murdering me, but just as capable of enjoying it.

"If I help you do it, then I wouldn't be a witness. I would be an accomplice. Just tell me how I can help. I'll do anything you need."

The smile that spread across Tyrell's face then should have been warning enough. It should have sent me racing from the room, out of the hotel, straight to the police. I knew he was a sadist. He didn't hide it or deny it. He wanted me to know it. So, I should have known that whatever he had me do in exchange for watching him stalk and murder someone would be something that would scar me.

16

TYRELL WAS ON THE PHONE. HIS CONVERSATION WAS BRIEF, and disturbing.

"I'm hungry, Byrd."

I couldn't hear the other side of the conversation, just snippets of words and syllables spoken rapidly, nervously.

Tyrell was lying beside me, still naked. I watched in amazement as his cock stiffened and lengthened. Whatever the man on the phone was telling him was arousing him.

"Send me the intel. And Byrd, no more fuckups. I would hate to have to replace you."

He hung up the phone and licked his lips.

"Turn over," he said.

"Why?" I asked.

Wrong question. Tyrell flipped me over, then dragged me across his lap. The impact of his rough palm upon my naked ass stung like a whip, but had the thudding, concussive power of a hammer blow. Surprisingly, it hurt even worse than when he'd lashed me with his belt.

I tried to squirm off of his lap, but that just made him strike me harder. His hand felt like a wooden paddle. He added deep bruises to the welts already covering my ass. After less than a minute of being spanked, I was sobbing, blubbering like a scolded toddler.

If I was expecting my tears to win me a reprieve, I was mistaken. The harder I sobbed, the harder he spanked me. By the time he finally released me, I was crying ugly, snot bubbling from my nose, saliva drooling from my mouth. But I felt something else as well. I felt floaty, a calm almost euphoric feeling, like I'd had one too many cups of wine. The pain had obviously released a shitload of endorphins, and I was soaring on them, high as fuck. I surprised myself, scared myself, by how much I enjoyed the feeling. My body was betraying me.

What the fuck is wrong with me?

I scrambled across the mattress, scurrying away from him, until Tyrell's words froze me.

"Lie still! On your belly."

I flattened out, face down on the mattress. When I felt Tyrell stir, I turned my head slightly so I could watch him. Tyrell stood. His erection hadn't diminished during my punishment. In fact, it was even larger, harder. My torment had excited him.

He reached out and patted my ass lightly, sending ripples through my flesh and making my ass jiggle. I flinched, still sobbing, feeling humiliated. I was mortified, imagining how my fat ass must look to him, but he gave no indication that he was anything but pleased.

"Shh," Tyrell said, rubbing my ass softly. His deep, resonant voice was warm and soothing, where it had previously been harsh and terrifying.

I began to relax. Tyrell's touch, when he wasn't causing me pain, had a calming effect on me. I stopped crying, stopped worrying about the cascade of ripples going

Fight For Me

through the twin globes of my buttocks each time he rubbed or patted them. It had probably been far worse when he was spanking me. Any modesty I had left fled me with that realization. Tyrell had completely exposed me, laid my insecurities bare, and I had known him less than twenty-four hours.

"You are beautiful," Tyrell said, in that deep, rumbling voice of his, and I believed it. I believed he thought I was, even if I did not believe I was.

I almost fell asleep as Tyrell caressed my ass, hips, and thighs, occasionally giving them a hard squeeze or a smack, but mostly just rubbing them, lavishing his attention upon the parts of my body I was the most self-conscious of. I was still too self-critical to fully relax, and too traumatized. I was expecting Tyrell to hurt me again at any moment. When I felt Tyrell's wet finger slip between my buttocks and into my anus, I let out a yelp and tried to sit up, but Tyrell placed a hand between my shoulder blades and shoved me violently back down to the bed.

Tyrell laid on top of me, kissing my shoulders where he had bitten them the night before. I felt his erection pressing against the cleft of my ass, and I knew what was about to happen. Tyrell sat up, licked his palm, then slathered his engorged cock with saliva. He was about to penetrate me anally, without any lubricant but his spit, just as Armando had. But Tyrell was much, much larger than Armando had been. I braced for the intrusion, but there was nothing that could have prepared me for the stomach churning agony as he burrowed into my guts and began thrusting, grunting and growling in my ear.

I wept again. This time it wasn't as much the pain and humiliation as it was the certainty that I was trapped. I had placed myself in a situation I couldn't get out of, with a person I could never escape from, never overcome. I wanted to call Becca, to beg for her help. But, I was certain that I would only be putting her life in danger as well.

Tyrell bit down on the back of my neck as he continued thrusting deep into my bowels. His thrusts pummeled me, hammered me into the mattress. I felt used, exploited, like an object, just a hole for him to fill. It was degrading, humiliating, and yet ... it was exciting. Exhilarating! Despite my shame, or perhaps because of it, I felt an orgasm begin to build.

I had heard of women who had orgasms during anal sex, but I had always assumed it was an urban myth, like handsome men with good jobs who were faithful, cooked, and did laundry and dishes. Men had prostate glands. But, to the best of my knowledge, women did not. Was my arousal strictly psychological? Had I become such a glutton for domination that just the act of being manhandled was enough to bring me to climax?

I was still musing over this when Tyrell's massive hand wrapped around my throat again and began to squeeze. That's when the orgasm reached its apex and exploded out of me with a scream. Tyrell continued to batter my sore anus to his own cataclysmic eruption.

When it was over, we both lay on our backs, trying to catch our breath, panting from the exertion. A smile split Tyrell's hardened features, and his diminishing erection stirred once more.

"Let's go kill someone," he said.

And, of all the shameful things I have confessed to myself throughout this ordeal, the perverse desires and immoral thoughts I have admitted that have caused me to reassess my image of myself as a decent human being, I am not ashamed at all of the physical reaction those words stirred in me. Tyrell was a predator, and he was also now my protector, and my mate. On the most primal level, I was eager to see another show of his dominance and strength, to prove he was worthy of me, that he was the superior breeding stock my very DNA called out for. I wanted to see him kill again, and then, I wanted him to kill for me.

Tyrell pulled a black, double-breasted suit from the closet, a v-neck black t-shirt, black boxers, and black socks. He wore black, ankle-length, leather boots with rubber soles. The suit, he explained, was made of a water resistant, moisture-wicking, wrinkle-proof, stain proof, stretchy, breathable material.

"The company that made it had a guy run a marathon while wearing the suit to prove how well it moved. I won't be running any marathons today, but I will need to move. And blood washes right off of it," Tyrell said.

"I don't think I have the right clothes for this."

"There's a pants suit in the closet. I had the concierge's desk bring it up last night while you were unconscious, along with a few other outfits. There's also a pair of jungle boots in there that are your size."

I should have known he would have thought of everything. The pinstriped pantsuit Tyrell had selected for me to wear wasn't breathable or moisture-wicking like Tyrell's. It was just a regular cotton/spandex blend. It was tight-fitting, but the spandex made it flexible enough that it was still pretty comfortable. Again, I was self-conscious about wearing something so form-fitting. I didn't even wear clothes that tight in the gym. But Tyrell's lustful gaze removed all the negative thoughts from my mind. It wasn't important what I thought I looked like. All that mattered was what Tyrell thought, and he clearly approved.

We dressed quickly, stealing glances at each other like

horny teenagers. Tyrell removed a gun-metal-gray suitcase from the closet, laid it on the bed, and opened it. As I expected, it contained two big revolvers, .44 calibers from the look of them, and a big serrated knife that looked like a prop from an 80's action film. He took the two revolvers and handed me the knife.

"I don't get a gun?"

Tyrell just smiled.

"You won't need it."

Tyrell slid another suitcase from beneath the bed. This one had two more handguns, automatics with oversized clips. There was a long tanto knife in there as well. Tyrell took the tanto knife, then slid the suitcase with the guns back under the bed. When we left the room, he put the "Do Not Disturb" sign on the door.

The driver from the previous evening was waiting for us when we left the hotel. He looked at me quizzically as he held open the door to the black sedan for Tyrell and I to enter. Before closing the car door, he knelt down to address Tyrell.

"Will I be dropping the young lady off somewhere along the way?" he asked in a way that was more of a suggestion than a question.

Tyrell shook his head slowly, his fierce, withering gaze fixing on the old driver, who shocked me by meeting it with little visible fear. He was clearly more than he appeared to be. A man comfortable with violence and, apparently, at peace with his own mortality.

"She will be joining the feast this evening," Tyrell responded. The driver nodded, then closed the door, walked around the car, and climbed behind the wheel. He never asked where we were going. Whoever "Byrd" was, he had not only arranged for the driver to be there, he had also

Fight For Me 111

given him whatever instructions he needed to fulfill the job. It occurred to me that I was the only one in the car who was completely in the dark. All I knew was someone was going to be killed. Who, Why, Where, and How remained a mystery. And I really didn't care.

We pulled up in front of a white brick building with accents of orange and yellow slate. It looked like a piece of modern art, clean and sterile with sharp angles. Tyrell studied the building like he was a mathematician solving a complex equation.

"Should I drive to the side exit, sir?" The driver asked.

"A few more minutes," Tyrell said. He looked up and down the street, focusing on the cars parked on the street, pedestrians strolling by, reserving the most intense scrutiny for a group of young millennials loitering in front of the building.

They looked out of place for the neighborhood. Hipsters with shaggy beards and skinny jeans. I would have never considered them a threat. They didn't look like cops or what I imagined gangsters would look like. They just looked like a bunch of potheads. College dropouts living in their parents' basement, or trust-fund babies wasting their parents' money to extend the party beyond their frat years. But I wasn't the professional, and something about them was obviously bothering Tyrell.

The doorman, dressed in a long red wool coat, wearing shiny black shoes, black slacks with razor sharp creases, and what looked like a navy admiral's cap, stepped out of the lobby as a limousine pulled to a stop in front of the building. He walked up to the vehicle and opened the door for the disheveled looking twenty-somethings to pile in. As they drove off, Tyrell finally relaxed. I couldn't imagine how stressful it had to be to remain that vigilant, that preternaturally cautious, all the time, to always have to consider the possibility that even a group of harmless-looking losers might be hired assassins or federal agents in disguise.

"Okay. Now we can go. Take one more drive around the block."

After another look at the building from all sides that were visible from the street, we parked in an alley on the side of the building. Tyrell didn't wait for the driver to open his door for him. He stepped out of the car and held out his hand for me to join him. This was it. Go time.

"Wait for us in back of the building by the rear exit," Tyrell said.

The driver nodded. I wondered how one went about finding a chauffeur who could do double duty as a getaway driver and be trusted to keep his mouth shut? Obviously, the old guy knew exactly what Tyrell and I were going into that building to do. And, by driving us to and from the crime scene, he would be legally complicit in the crime. I wondered how much he was getting paid to risk thirty years to life for conspiracy to commit murder? For that matter, I wondered how much Tyrell was getting paid? I would have to ask him some time. After the job was done.

We went through the side door, which led to a hallway with a service elevator.

"This is the only elevator that goes all the way up to the top floor without needing a key. It won't get us into the penthouse, but it will get us to the door."

"Then what?"

"Then you ring the doorbell, and ask for Jimmy. But first ..." Tyrell grabbed me by the frilly white blouse he'd selected for me to wear beneath the pinstriped pants suit. He undid two more buttons so that my breasts were practically spilling

Fight For Me 113

out of it. Tyrell paused, took a step back, appraising my voluptuous curves in that tight-fitting pants-suit with my shirt unbuttoned revealing what looked like half a yard of cleavage. But Tyrell wasn't satisfied. He wanted the entire yard. He stepped forward and undid another button.

"There. Now he'll definitely open the door."

"But what if I'm not his type?"

"You aren't," Tyrell said. "But, you are beautiful. Even if you aren't his type, he can't ignore that. He'll at least be curious."

Tyrell had called me beautiful. He'd said it casually, as a matter of course, a simple fact rather than a compliment or an attempt at flattery. Somehow, that made it far more special.

"I don't think everyone would consider me beautiful," I said.

"Two nights ago, men were beating the shit out of each other for the opportunity to sniff your panties. None of them knew anything about you. They weren't doing it because of your personality. They were doing it because you are gorgeous. And your modesty, while endearing, feels more like insecurity. This isn't the time for insecurity, you understand me?"

I nodded.

Tyrell seized me by the jaw and forced me to look at him.

"Fucking answer me when I talk to you!"

"Y-yes. Yes, I understand."

"Yes, who?"

"Yes, Master."

"And, besides, if he hasn't been laid already tonight ... well..."

"Pussy is pussy," I continued for him, filling in the blanks.

Tyrell nodded, smiling as he released his grip on my face.

"Yes. Pussy is pussy." Tyrell stepped closer. He reached between my legs, cupping my sex. "But this, this pussy is mine. That makes it special. And I will protect what's mine. So, don't worry about anything. You are safe. From now on, you will always be safe."

And just like that, I wasn't worried anymore. Not even a little bit. Tyrell was my champion, my hero, my master. He had already proven himself to me. With him at my side, I was completely fearless, perhaps even reckless. I didn't know what I was walking into, and I didn't care. I was with my master, hunting, about to take down prey together, and that's all that mattered at that moment.

During the brief ride up to the penthouse, Tyrell changed the plan. He wanted me to be the one to make the kill.

"He has a bodyguard who may or may not be in there with him. I'll need to handle the bodyguard. You handle the meal."

"Does that mean I get a gun now?"

"I told you, you won't need it."

As the elevator reached the top floor and the doors whooshed open, Tyrell removed the two big revolvers from the shoulder holsters he wore under his suit jacket. I reached inside my jacket and grabbed the hilt of the big bowie knife my Master had given me. I tried to imagine actually using it, plunging it into someone's chest. I wasn't completely certain I could do it, but I didn't want to disappoint Tyrell.

He put a hand on top of mine, gently seizing my wrist, and pulled it out of my jacket and away from the knife.

"You can't knock on the door with your hand in your jacket. You'll look like you've come there to murder him."

"I was just touching it. Making sure I can get to it quickly."

"You'll get to it fast enough. And, I'll be right behind you."

Tyrell nudged me forward and stepped aside so he would not be visible to anyone looking out of the door. I knocked and waited. There was no response. I turned to look at Tyrell who nodded again toward the door. I knocked again, harder this time. Still no response. I knocked a third time, banging on the door like the Gestapo.

"Who is it?"

The voice was deep and husky. It had to come from a much larger man than the one Tyrell had described to me.

"The agency sent me," I said.

"What?"

"The agency sent me," I repeated.

The door opened up. A huge black man, not as tall but at least a hundred pounds heavier than Tyrell, stood in the doorway. He looked annoyed at first, then his eyes softened and clouded with lust.

"Oh, okay. Come on in, momma. Hey, Dennis! Dennis! The girl you ordered just got here!"

I took several steps inside the door. The big bodyguard closed it behind me. Tyrell was still outside. A skinny white guy with a blond pompadour staggered out of the bedroom into the great room, wearing nothing but boxer shorts. White powder coated both nostrils, and there was vomit in his mustache.

"I didn't order any bitches tonight."

"She said the agency sent her over. You must have called while you were high."

"I'm always high. Still, I'd remember ordering a whore. And why would I order a fat bitch? I don't like fat bitches."

The big bouncer laughed. He was directly behind me, and he reached around and cupped my titties in his enormous hands.

"Well, I like her. She's got great tits."

"Then you fuck her. But I ain't paying for her."

I turned in the bouncer's arms, looking back at the locked apartment door, expecting to see it burst open and Tyrell to come storming in with guns blazing. But there was not so much as a gentle knock. I was on my own. I wondered if this was some sort of test.

"How about I fuck you both," I said, getting back into character. The lawyer was too far away, and all I had was a knife. If I could at least get him closer to me, I could stab the big bouncer and then get the lawyer before he could run.

I wriggled free of the bouncer and took a few steps toward the lawyer, unbuttoning my top, and allowing my breasts to spill free of my blouse.

"See, I told you she had great tits. Look at those big motherfuckers. Goddamn!"

The lawyer turned away, shaking his head, and waving me away dismissively.

"Nah, I told you. I ain't into fat bitches. Her tits are too big."

"Maybe your dick is just too small!" I shouted.

The lawyer turned to me with a malevolent sneer on his face.

"What the fuck did you just say to me, whore?"

He was across the room, within arm's reach, in a few short strides. He reached out and grabbed me by the jaw.

Fight For Me 117

That's when I sank the blade in beneath his sternum as deep as it would go, driving upward toward the vicinity of his heart. I wrenched the knife free and stabbed him again and again.

"I said, who the fuck are you calling fat, you short dick piece of shit!"

The lawyer's eyes widened with shock and pain, then fixed in place and glazed over. I stabbed him twice more as I heard the bouncer cry out behind me.

"Hey! What the fuck are you doing to him?"

I heard his heavy footsteps running up in back of me. I pulled the knife out of the lawyer's chest and let his limp body fall to my feet as I turned to face the huge bouncer, who was struggling to jerk his gun free from his shoulder holster. The bouncer's huge biceps and massive lats made the maneuver more difficult than it should have been. He didn't seem to possess the requisite flexibility to accomplish the task. I wondered how he ever managed to wipe his own ass.

Everything felt as if it had slowed down to a sluggish half-speed while I stood there calculating how fast I would have to be to stab this man to death before he shot me or knocked me down with his forward momentum. That's when the front door finally burst open and Tyrell walked in.

"Hey, fat boy. Leave my woman alone."

Tyrell was pointing his two big revolvers at the bodyguard, who had yet to clear his weapon from his shoulder holster. The man turned to face Tyrell and immediately threw up his hands.

"Look, man. I'm cool. Dennis is already dead, man. I ain't tryin'a follow him. I ain't no hero. As far as I'm concerned, I didn't see a damn thing."

Tyrell smiled. His gaze drifted past the big bodyguard to

fix on me. He nodded. That was all. Just a nod. We hadn't discussed any codes or signals, but, all the same, I knew exactly what he wanted me to do. I leapt up onto the bodyguard's back, wrapping my legs around his substantial waist, and with the knife still wet with his employer's blood, ripped the serrated blade across the big man's throat.

The bodyguard stumbled forward, clutching his lacerated throat. I slid off his back and took my place beside my master, watching the big man die. I had cut both his carotid artery and jugular vein along with his windpipe. He would not only bleed to death, he would drown in his own blood, gasping for oxygen. It was a horrible way to go. I was transfixed by his agony, his desperation as he clawed at the walls and then the carpet, struggling for air. When he finally lay still, I waited for the wave of guilt I knew I would feel, but nothing came.

"Stay by my side," Tyrell said, he was still holding the two revolvers, and I sensed that he was on alert. His eyes scanned the apartment, and his head was slightly tilted, listening for something.

"Are we leaving now?"

"Shhhhhh!"

"What is it?" I whispered.

"This isn't the bodyguard he was with the other night. There must be two of them."

And that meant the other one must still be in the apartment, probably waiting to ambush us. I knew what Tyrell was thinking. If the guy was in here hiding somewhere, he might have seen our faces. And if we left, he might follow us and try to shoot us in our backs. He had to be dealt with.

"Fucking Byrd. This was his last chance," Tyrell growled. He gave me a quick glance. "No witnesses," he said, need-

Fight For Me

lessly. That was already understood. I didn't want to go to jail either.

I gestured toward the bedroom the lawyer had come out of. Tyrell motioned for me to stay behind him. I did as I was told, standing in the living room between two dead bodies. Tyrell stepped through the bedroom door, pointing his revolvers. I stayed back in the main room as I had been told – until I heard the sound of a grown man begging for his life.

"Hey, man. It's cool! It's cool, bruh! I didn't see anything! I didn't see anything! You ain't got to kill me, brother. I ain't see shit!"

Then I heard him scream.

"NOOoooooo! Arrrrlllllllgh!"

It didn't sound like the man was putting up much of a fight. The entire encounter was over in seconds. Tyrell came out of the bedroom, wiping off his tanto knife with a throw pillow.

"Let's go," he said.

Before we left, he took a photograph of the dead lawyer with his cellphone. I felt both sick and oddly elated, proud, looking down at the lawyer's eviscerated corpse. I had made a mess of him. There were at least half a dozen stab wounds in his chest and abdomen. Blood had soaked the carpet around him. Tyrell guided me around the widening pond of red plasma. I followed him out the door and into the elevator.

"What took you so long to come in? I thought you were right behind me? They almost got me," I said.

"No. They didn't. You took care of them, just like I knew you would. I was right outside the door. No one was going to hurt you."

I couldn't really dispute that. He had been there when I needed him.

"How did it feel?"

"I feel like I just took a bump of speed. My heart is about to beat right out of my chest!"

Tyrell's face hardened.

"You don't take drugs, do you?"

The elevator reached the bottom floor. The doors wafted open, and Tyrell did not move. He continued to pin me in place with his cold gaze.

"I – I mean I have. I experimented in high school, like everyone else. But I haven't done that in years."

Tyrell held the elevator doors open with his left arm, but had not made a motion to leave. His eyes explored my face, searching for the lie. But I was telling the truth. I was clean.

"There are rules. And the first one is that you will not use any drugs. You understand?"

"I am not on drugs."

Tyrell seized my face in his hand, the same way that lawyer had. For a moment, I had the fleeting urge to pull the knife from where I had replaced it under my suit jacket and plunge it into Tyrell's chest. I doubted my ability to accomplish such a feat. Most likely, Tyrell would have taken it from me and made me eat it. I trembled, and a tear wept from my eye. I had almost forgotten who Tyrell was, what he was capable of. He was a killer. A man who murdered people for money. We'd known each other for less than 48 hours. I knew almost nothing about him. As easily as he'd dispatched that bodyguard, he could have done the same to me.

"Yes, Master. I understand."

He released me, and together we walked out the back service entrance of the hotel, where our driver was waiting.

Fight For Me

He looked nervous, agitated, a little annoyed, but he remained silent.

"Home," Tyrell commanded as we slid onto the back seat.

The driver nodded and stepped on the accelerator, piloting us out of the alley and onto the main street, back toward our hotel.

17

———

TYRELL MADE LOVE TO ME. IN HIS OWN INDELICATE WAY, HE poured out his emotions through his flesh. He bit me and choked me while he filled my sopping wet pussy with his engorged cock, but he whispered to me the entire time, telling me how proud he was of me, how wonderful it was to have someone he could trust. I came as much from the sound of his voice, the emotion in his words, as I did from the relentless, piston-like pounding of his cock against my cervix.

Afterward, Tyrell held me tight against him. I played the entire evening over and over in my mind. My fear when the door closed and I was alone in the hotel room with the two strange men. Tyrell had been right. I was a trained fighter. I had a knife, the element of surprise. I had come there prepared to kill, and I had one of the most dangerous men on the planet only a few feet away, behind a cheap wooden door. Master. My protector. I'd had nothing to fear.

"So, what happens now?"

"Now, we sleep," Tyrell replied.

"I mean with us?"

"I know what you meant. We can talk about it in the morning."

"Are you leaving? Now that your job is over? Are you going to leave me?"

The idea terrified me for some reason. It wasn't just that Tyrell was everything I could have hoped for in a man, and a lot more I'd never dreamed of, it was the fact that I had killed two men. What if the police traced the bodies back to me somehow? Would I have to face it alone? And what about the guilt I knew would eventually hit me? I had taken two lives, and been an accomplice in the death of another. There would be emotional consequences for that. Would I have to face that alone too?

"No," Tyrell answered. He didn't elaborate, and I didn't push. I didn't dare. He said we would talk about it in the morning, so I took him at his word. His reassurance that he would not abandon me was all I needed for now.

That night, I slept like a babe in its mother's arms. I dreamt about a future with Tyrell. A future awash with blood.

When I woke to the sound of my Master running a bath, the sun was already streaming into the hotel room. Tyrell was on the phone with someone I assumed was Byrd.

"You aren't fired, and I'm not going to kill you, but that's twice you made mistakes on this job. I need an explanation or there will be punishment."

I slipped from the sheets and walked toward him, but Tyrell held up a finger, signaling for me to wait. I stopped and didn't move. My Master was listening intently to the phone. I could vaguely hear a panicky, squeaky, whining voice, speaking quickly, talking for his survival. I wanted to laugh, but the seriousness of my Master's expression stifled the chuckle before it could materialize and wiped the smirk

Fight For Me   125

from my face. I remained still, unmoving, waiting for my Master's command. He was in a mood, and I knew it wasn't wise to anger him.

Tyrell was still talking, or rather he was listening, and growling his disapproval from time to time, occasionally nodding, as if Byrd could see the gesture through the phone. He walked over to me, took my hand, and led me over to the tub.

"I'm going now. Find me another job in a few days. Make it something local. Yes, I mean here. In this town. I'm staying here for a while. Yes. That's what I said. I'm staying here. This isn't open for discussion. Are you arguing with me? I didn't think so. Just fucking find me something."

Tyrell looked at me and smiled. My heart felt lighter. My Master was staying – at least for a few days. He guided me into the tub and began washing me with a soapy sponge, removing the smell of his sweat and semen from my skin and replacing it with the scent of lavender and roses. I could not tell which scent I preferred, but I was definitely sad for the last vestiges of the evening's passion to be scrubbed from my skin. It felt like losing him. But there would be many more evenings like last night. Wouldn't there?

"Master?"

"You may call me Sir if you prefer."

A smile split my face.

"Okay, I prefer Master. But Sir probably works better in public. Rolls off the tongue a little easier too."

Master nodded.

"Can we talk now? I mean, about what happens next?"

My Master stopped washing me and leaned down to peer into my eyes. He caressed my cheek gently with his fingertips, the way one would touch a newborn.

"We are going to find us a house. You will live there. I

will train you to be my companion, my assistant, my apprentice. To do what I do. Sometimes I will have to leave you, and you will stay in the house. Sometimes I will take you with me on assignments."

He sat back and resumed washing me. He did not ask for my input, nor did he ask for my approval. He had decided that this is how it would be. So, this is how it would be.

When he finished cleaning me, then drying me with the softest, fluffiest towel I'd ever felt, he told me to get dressed, then called Byrd again.

"I need a realtor. A discreet one. Tell her to be at the hotel in one hour. I also want a vehicle. What's the fastest car they make that will comfortably accommodate someone my size? Sounds good. Have it delivered to the hotel. I need a new driver's license and passport also. Make sure the car is registered to the new identity. Oh, and, Byrd. A new passport and driver's license for her too. Don't test me, Byrd. You know who 'her' is. Just do it!" He slammed down the phone and began getting dressed.

I wanted to ask him about my job, the hair salon, and my apartment. Did he really expect me to abandon it all? Is that what I signed up for? The new life my Master spelled out for me sounded exciting, like a psychopath's version of a fairytale. My version. But did that mean I had to burn my past completely? Did this new life require the total death of my old one? What about Becca? Before I could stop myself, I was asking questions, terrified they might be answered the way I assumed they must.

"I – I have a friend ..."

Tyrell, my Master, paused in the middle of buttoning up a crisp new white shirt and raised an eyebrow, turning his head toward me.

"A boyfriend?"

Fight For Me **127**

"No – no, nothing like that. She's my oldest friend. I can't just disappear on her. I need to talk to her. She'll be worried. And I have to figure out what to do with my apartment and my job at the salon."

Tyrell resumed buttoning his shirt. He bent down and picked up a black tie and began tying it in a perfect Windsor knot as he spoke.

"We will go to your apartment and get anything of sentimental value, anything that cannot be easily replaced. You won't talk to anyone. Not your neighbors or your landlord. No one. You will just get your stuff and leave. People disappear all the time. Your job, the salon, will keep your chair for you for a few weeks, a month maybe. Then, when it's clear you aren't coming back, they'll rent it to someone else. Your friends will be concerned, suspicious. They might even go to the police, but I doubt it. They will think you just moved on without saying goodbye. They'll be hurt, angry, but then they'll get over it. Once or twice a year, when they run into each other at parties or at the coffee shop, they'll ask if anyone ever heard from you. Maybe they'll tell a few rumors about you marrying some rich guy who whisked you away to Paris, or moving to Hollywood to become an actress, or getting hooked on heroine and becoming a street whore, but no one will really know. And, eventually, they'll stop asking, stop mentioning your name at all. Some new scandal or drama will take your place, and they will forget all about you."

His words chilled me. He wasn't threatening me, but it was clear he was letting me know he could make me disappear and no one would come looking for me. But he was wrong. Becca would come.

"Becca wouldn't forget. She'd never forget, and she'd never stop looking for me. That's why I have to tell her something. Obviously, I'm not going to tell her I decided to shack up with a hitman and become his apprentice. But I have to tell her something."

Tyrell finished tying his tie and slipped on his black sports jacket. He looked exactly what you would imagine a hitman would look like. It was way too on the nose, but it worked for him.

Tyrell tossed me my phone. "Then tell her something."

I dialed Becca's number and felt my hands tremble and a heat flush my cheeks. I had been an asshole to her that last time we spoke. She'd had every right to be worried about me. She would have every right to be worried about me now. Nothing I was doing, or had done in the last three days, said much for my judgment or my sanity.

There was no reason for her to forgive me, but I knew she would. I knew she always would. Just like I knew she'd come looking for me if I disappeared, and that finding me would put her life in peril. She loved me. She truly loved me. And I loved her, but I knew I wasn't worthy of this love. The adoration in her eyes made me feel like a fraud, an imposter. Rather than lift my self-esteem, her love ground it underfoot, crushed my ego beneath the weight of her lofty expectations. I rathered my Master's cruelty to her fawning adoration.

"Hello?"

I wanted to hang up, but I had begged for the opportunity to speak to her, and I knew that hanging up would make her even more suspicious, more likely to come after me, more likely to end up dead.

"It's me."

"Athena?"

"How've you been?"

Fight For Me 129

"How've I been? I'm not the one you should be worried about."

"Look, I'm sorry about how all of that went down."

There was silence on the other end of the phone.

"Becca?"

"I'm still here."

"Well? Say something?"

"I don't know what you expect me to say. I don't know you anymore, Athena."

"Bullshit, Becca. You got scared, and I don't blame you. Shit got out of hand. But, you're still my girl, right? Right?"

"I don't know, Athena. I mean, you know I love you. That's never going to change."

"I love you too, Becca. And I need to know we're okay. I need you to tell me we're still cool."

"What happened that night?"

Now, it was my turn to pause.

"Did you find your champion? The man of your dreams? Your master?"

I knew that answering that question would only hurt Becca. So, instead, I changed the subject.

"How's Trish?"

"What do you mean? I thought she was staying with you?" Becca said.

"I haven't been back to my apartment in a couple days. You haven't heard from her?"

"Nope. I've been busy at the salon."

"I've been busy too. Would you check on her for me?"

"Why can't you check on her? Why haven't you been home?"

"Listen, Becca. I'm going to be going away for a little while. I – I met someone."

This time the silence crashed down like an avalanche, smothering them both.

"Who? The guy who broke Dillon's arm?"

And killed David, but Becca didn't know that.

"It – it's complicated."

"Complicated? That guy's a psychopath!"

She had no idea.

"You don't know him, Becca. He's – he's ..." There weren't really words for what Tyrell was. Not words Becca would understand. Alpha. Dominant. Master. Murderer. They were all true, but none of them told the entire story. "Becca, it's what I want. Please. I'm not asking you to understand, just try to be happy for me. I'm happy, Becca. I really am."

"I love you, Athena. You know that. And, as much as it kills me, as much as you don't fucking deserve it, I'll be here for you when this guy hurts you, if he doesn't kill you."

"Thank you, Becca."

"And I'll check on Trish."

I hung up the phone, feeling sad about Becca. The conversation had felt so final. Maybe I was the asshole she thought I was.

Master's phone rang just as he'd finished tying his tie, a black silk one with black paisleys, and slipping on a sports jacket.

"Do you ever wear any color other than black?"

"My shirt is white," he said, then picked up his phone and answered it. This time, he didn't say a word. He listened, then hung up, tucking the phone in the inside pocket of his sports jacket. "Our car is here."

I liked how he said "our." I loved how he had so completely claimed me. He took my hand, and together we walked out of the hotel room and down the hall to the elevator. When we reached the lobby, I took note of how Tyrell's eyes systematically scanned the room from floor to ceiling, person to person, shadow to shadow. I wondered if this was what his life was always like? Constant vigilance. Never letting his guard down. Never truly relaxing. Was this truly what I wanted?

We strolled through the lobby. As we walked, with my Master still scrutinizing every gesture, every change in expression, from everyone within eyesight, hand gripping mine tightly, I wondered what would happen if someone were to start shooting at us? Would my Master protect me, or use me as a human shield? I believed Tyrelll would protect me, but I couldn't entirely rule out being used as a shield. I was surprised by how little that realization disturbed me.

Outside, a man in a blue suit with a money-green tie stood by a brand new, black (of course) Mercedes AMG GT 63 S. He smiled and stepped forward with his hand outstretched, holding keys.

"Mister Thompson?"

Tyrell nodded, and the keys to a brand new one hundred and forty thousand dollar, six hundred and thirty horse-power, luxury sedan were placed in his hand without him so much as showing an ID or signing a receipt. The man simply handed over the keys, bowed slightly, then stepped to the curb to hail a taxi. Tyrell opened my car door; there was a driver's license and a passport on both the passenger and driver's side seats. I guess that's why the guy hadn't asked for any identification. He was providing it.

I sat down and quickly scooped up my passport, eager to see who I would be from now on. The passport had a photo of me that looked like it had been taken from my actual passport. How the hell had they gotten that photo? I wondered briefly, before I saw the name. Scarlet Thompson. As Tyrell closed my door and made his way around the vehicle to the driver's side, I snuck a peek at his passport Tiberius Thompson. Our new identities were man and wife.

Tyrell scooped up the passport and driver's license, glanced at both quickly, then tucked them away in his pocket. I couldn't stop staring at mine. The driver's license photo was also the photo from my actual driver's license. I wasn't in love with the name Scarlet. It sounded like the name of some James Bond heroine. I loved the idea of being Tyrell's wife, even if it was all a lie.

We had only been sitting in the car for a minute or two when an immaculately dressed, quaffed, and manicured woman in her late forties or fifties, wearing a light blue Chanel business suit, stepped up to the car. My Master unlocked the passenger door and gestured for her to get in.

"Hi, my name is Brenda. I'm here to show you a few houses. What are we looking for?"

"At least four acres, one road on or off the property, visible from any room in the front of the house. Within 30 minutes of town, but outside local jurisdiction. Preferably wind and solar powered, with a well, a hundred percent off-grid."

"Size? Number of bedrooms? Number of baths?"

"I have no preference," My Master answered, then looked over at me.

"Three bedroom, two and a half baths, with a study, and a game room slash exercise room, and maybe a pool, and a large kitchen with granite countertops"

"Budget?"

"Unlimited," Tyrell replied.

Brenda typed all of our criterion into a real estate app on her phone. There were only seven houses that came close to

Fight For Me 133

meeting all of our requirements, and one of them was so dilapidated just looking at it made me sad.

"We aren't in the market for a fixer upper," Tyrell said, and Brenda immediately removed two more homes from the list. That left only four options. Brenda gave us directions, and Tyrell drove us out of the city, to the first house on the list. It was a single-story, Spanish-style home, orangish brown stucco and brown, tan, and orange slate stone. Three bell towers, red clay roof tiles, ornate wrought-iron gates opening onto a series of arched corridors supported by square pillars, and windows with brown vinyl frames that had a smoky rust-colored tint. It sat on ten acres, and there was even a vineyard and a basement with a wine cellar. I was immediately smitten with it, but the choice wasn't mine.

Tyrell walked the perimeter of the house, looking at the road, the surrounding trees, and even the hills off in the distance. He went inside and did the same, barely looking at the interior of the house, just walking from window to window, looking out at the road.

"We would need to cut back those trees," Tyrell said, pointing at a copse of oaks and evergreens.

"They're so pretty, though," I said.

"It's either the trees or the house," he said.

"You haven't even looked at the house."

"Do you like it?"

"I love it!"

"That's good enough for me. How much?"

The real estate agent, Brenda, was in the middle of texting someone, and didn't hear my Master's question. I knew he wasn't inclined to repeat himself, and I knew how dangerous his temper could be.

"He asked how much the house costs?"

"This one is one-point-eight," Brenda said.

"Million?"

"Yes, ma'am. One-point-eight million. It's a steal for this area."

"We'll take it. But first, the seller has to remove those trees," my Master said.

Brenda looked over at me, and I shrugged, then nodded my consent, hoping my Master didn't see the gesture and think I was somehow undermining his authority.

"Okay, I'll let the seller know."

"We'd like to close by the end of the week."

Brenda paused.

"We can't close on a loan that quickly."

Tyrell shook his head.

"No loan. Cash. End of the week, and I want those trees gone."

18

THE NEXT TWO MONTHS PASSED LIKE A BLUR. TYRELL ALLOWED me to decorate the house, but he had to approve every selection, right down to the color of the bath towels. I picked out all the furniture and appliances online, and he had them delivered and installed. For more than sixty days, we never left the property. He said he wanted to make sure we were in sync before we went back out into the world.

Occasionally, Byrd would call with a job for Tyrell. He always turned him down, telling him "we" weren't ready yet. But Byrd was persistent. He must have called every week for the last six. But, each time, my Master's answer was the same. Not yet.

My Master worked with me on my skills every day, making me a better fighter, a more efficient killer. First, he taught me new martial arts moves and techniques, then advanced to knives and guns. Finally, he combined them. He had a gun range installed on the property. And we would spar out there in the field then immediately pick up our guns and try to shoot targets a hundred yards away. I sucked at it. Most times, I missed the target entirely. Tyrell, on the other hand, shot nice, tight, little groupings, center-mass, on the human-shaped targets.

"How did you get so good at this, Sir?"

"Necessity."

"Seriously, Sir. Why don't you ever tell me about your past? Were you in the military?"

"No."

"FBI? CIA?"

"No."

"You don't learn to shoot like that just going to the local shooting range on the weekends, Sir."

Tyrell let out a long sigh, then paused.

"My father."

"Your father taught you how to shoot, Sir?"

"My father was in special forces in 'Nam. Later on, he was a member of the Black Panther Party. He helped train a lot of them in hand-to-hand combat and firearms. That's where he developed a lot of the techniques he used to train me. It was fun then. Training with all those brothers. I was the only kid out there. They treated me like their mascot. Most of them are dead now, though. Murdered by the police and the FBI. Not my dad, though. He survived all of that and just moved on to other areas where he could use his special skills. By the time I was in middle school, he was working for the mafia."

"Doing what, Sir?"

"What do you think?"

I nodded.

"So, it runs in the family, huh?"

Tyrell smiled, a sad, ironic expression devoid of all mirth, and shook his head.

"It's more complicated than that."

"Tell me, please, Sir."

Fight For Me 137

Tyrell looked up at the sky. His brow furrowed, and his smile disappeared. When his gaze landed on me again, his face was expressionless, a stone tablet.

"This drill we're doing? I have been doing these kinds of drills since elementary school. When other kids were learning to hit a baseball and ride a skateboard, I was learning how to field strip a Glock and sever major arteries with a Ka-Bar. By the time I was ten, I could do a hundred pullups and a thousand pushups."

I nodded. It explained so much.

"When did you ..."

"Kill for the first time?"

"Yeah."

"My dad was taking me to the playground. We never went to the playground. He walked me over to the basketball courts, and I thought he was going to show me how to play ball. He was dressed in shorts and a tank top. I almost never saw him without a shirt and tie, so I was excited. We were actually going to play.

"There were all these guys out there, older guys, like six-footers. They were good too. Flying through the air and dunking the ball. I was in awe. Then my dad left my side and sort of jogged out onto the court. I thought he was going to play ball with them. My dad was good at everything. At least, that's what I thought then. So, I was excited to see him show these guys up. In that brief moment, I pictured him leaping from the foul line like Dr. J and doing a reverse slam dunk. That's not what happened, though."

His voice trailed off and his eyes drifted upward again.

"What happened, Master?"

Master sighed, then focused on me again. There were storms in his eyes, something dark and violent brewing in those cold, green orbs. I wondered if it would be wiser to change the subject.

"He pulled out his gun and shot two of them. He shot them right there on the court in front of everyone. Then he just turned and walked back over to me. He wiped off the gun, ejected the clip, and tossed it away. He was almost back with me when he was tackled. There were three of them, and more coming. They were the guys' friends. My dad was fighting them off, breaking arms and legs, but more kept coming. During the scuffle, he must have dropped the extra magazine for his Glock. Because I saw it lying there on the ground, so I picked it up. Then I walked over to where my dad had tossed the gun, picked that up too, loaded the magazine into it, and went over to where my dad was fighting those guys, and I started firing. I hit the first guy twice in the back. Center mass. Just like my dad taught me. When he hit the ground, I put another one in his skull. I hit another guy in the chest, and another in the stomach. The rest started running. My dad took the gun from me and finished off the guy I'd shot in the stomach. He put one in the forehead of the guy I shot in the chest, even though he already looked dead to me."

"Then what happened, Sir?"

Master laughed.

"We went out for ice cream. He took me to get ice cream. He told me how proud he was of me, then bought me a sundae. Later on that day, he took me to the movies. We had McDonald's for dinner. That was the best day I can remember with my dad."

I didn't know what to say. This story told me so much more about who Tyrell was, but I didn't know what to do with the information. I wanted to hug him, comfort him, but I didn't know if we would allow it.

Fight For Me   139

"May I hug you, Master?"

Master looked shocked, then his face softened, and he opened his arms to me. I stepped forward, and we stood there, in the middle of the gun range, holding each other for what felt like an eternity. Then, Tyrell stepped away from me.

"Let's get back to work."

We trained all day, harder than usual. I was bruised and fatigued when we staggered back into the house. Well, I staggered, my Master was sweating, but otherwise looked no different than he had when we'd walked out there that morning. We hadn't even paused for lunch, so we were both ravenous.

"Get dressed. Something pretty. We're going out to dinner."

"Shower with me? Please, Master?"

Master and I peeled out of our workout clothes. I gathered them off the floor and carried them into the laundry room and threw them in the washer while Master started the shower. Master liked the water almost hot enough to blister skin, and I still wasn't quite used to it, but I never complained. This time, when I returned, the water was at a reasonable temperature. I smiled, knowing he'd done that for me.

I grabbed a washcloth and the black soap made from palm oil, shea butter, coconut oil, charcoal ash, and cocoa butter that master preferred, and began lathering the thick muscles on his chest, shoulders, back, and arms, working my way over his stomach and down his thighs and calves. My face was inches from his stiffening cock, and I paused to service him, taking him between my lips and down my throat, allowing him to fuck my throat without gagging. He lifted me up to my feet, then wrapped his arms around my waist and spun me so that my thighs were draped over his shoulders, my sex brushing against his lips. My head was facing downward, between his legs, and I took him in my mouth again as he began to lick and suck my clitoris in a standing "69".

With anyone else, I wouldn't have been able to relax in such a precarious position. I would have worried that they would drop me. But I trusted my Master absolutely. His tongue flicked rapidly across my clit. Occasionally, he paused to suck at my labia or plunge his tongue deep inside me, fucking me with it. I was still sucking his cock, and I could feel it swell in my mouth as he neared orgasm, and my own orgasm began to build. I grabbed his muscular buttocks and pulled him deeper into me, further down my throat. He rocked his hips back and forth to match the rhythm of my head bobbing up and down on his thick cock. His tongue blurred across my clit, eager to make me cum too. When my climax arrived, he thrust his tongue inside me and I contracted around it, simultaneously, his own orgasm filled my mouth, and I eagerly swallowed every drop. Not once did I worry about him losing control and dropping me. I had learned over the past month that Master was the very definition of control.

I finished washing Master, and then he washed me as well, pausing to hungrily suck at my nipples. Then, he left me alone in the shower to shampoo and condition my hair while he got dressed and called for reservations. When I was done washing and blow drying my hair, Master was already dressed in a gray pin-striped suit with a black shirt and black tie. He looked amazing. Of course, he had already selected the dress and shoes he wanted me to wear tonight: a short, form-fitting, low cut black dress that fit tight on my ass and was an inch from revealing my areolas.

Fight For Me 141

"Are you sure this is appropriate for dinner, Master?"

"It is if I say it is," he replied, and of course, he was right. His opinion was the only one that mattered. Not the other patrons of whatever restaurant we were going to. Not the host or hostess. Not the waiters. Not the chef. Not even my own opinion mattered. Only his.

"Put these on also," Master said, holding up two garters. One with a holster that contained a .22 Luger automatic, and the other that held a sheath with an arrow-shaped palm knife. Under his own jacket, he had a shoulder holster with twin .44 caliber revolvers. I wondered if these were just a precaution, or if Tyrell had something else planned beyond a romantic dinner.

I felt both sexy and dangerous as we walked out to the car, and Master held the door for me, as he always did. Together, we drove out of our private little compound for the first time in over a month. I had learned so much about the art of killing human beings during that time. I was physically stronger, mentally and emotionally powerful. And, my Master and I had grown so much closer. The drills we did every day had put us perfectly in sync. We now moved in harmony, like a choreographed dance. I was anxious to test us in real combat, but I also longed to just be out in public, enjoying the city, having a nice meal at a fancy restaurant like any normal couple.

The restaurant was a Michelin five-star, Asian fusion place that was designed like a Buddhist temple. The chef was a celebrity who had his own cooking show on a major cable network. We valet parked the Mercedes and walked past the long line, where the waiter showed us to a private dining area where only three other couples were seated. Our waiter was a tall, slender, Chinese American man with a big, welcoming smile and perfect English with no hint of an accent.

"Would you like to see our wine list?"

Master ordered a six-hundred-dollar bottle of sake made by a brewery called Takagi Shuzo. I'd never heard of it, but I'd only had sake a few times in my life, at all-you-can-eat sushi restaurants that served it for three or four-dollars a cup. This was an entirely new experience.

"What does it taste like to you?"

"It tastes like whiskey, but it has almost a fruity flavor. Like melons."

Master nodded, pleased with my answer. He ordered caviar and sushi, followed by Wagyu beef filets. It was the most incredible meal I'd ever had.

We skipped dessert and took a drive downtown to a smoky blues club that was once a speakeasy during the roaring twenties. A big, beautiful, black woman with hips, breasts, and ass that made my own look practically anorexic was belting out an old Bessie Smith tune about careless love while men and women of all ages danced, played pool, drank powerful mixed drinks with names like Voodoo Mama and Alabama Slamma, and smoked and vaped just about everything but tobacco. The air smelled like cloves, jasmine, and marijuana. Master took me out onto the dance floor, and we swayed to the music, embracing each other tightly. When the song ended, we took our seats, and Master's phone rang. I knew who it was, of course. Byrd was the only one who ever called. Master didn't seem to have anyone else in his life except me and Byrd.

"What? Okay. Send me the details. That's right. Send me the details." He hung up, then smiled across the table at me. "We have a new meal."

Fight For Me 143

"Meal", Master explained, was their code word for a hit, because it satiated his hunger for violence.

"I was in a foul mood one day. I hadn't had a job in a while. I told Byrd that I was starving for some violence, and he answered, 'Then let's get you a meal.' We've been calling it that ever since."

"So, who's our meal this time?"

"You'll like this one. An abusive husband. A gold-digging thug who married into a wealthy family. The woman's father has a fatal illness, prostate cancer that has metastasized into his organs. He doesn't want any of his money going into his son-in-law's pockets, but he doesn't want to cut his only daughter out of his will. He wants this guy gone before he dies. And he doesn't care how it happens. He would prefer that it didn't look like a professional hit. He wants something messy," Tyrell said. The delight in his eyes reminded me of how he'd looked during my little tournament, right before he broke Dillon's leg.

19

LEVI OTTUM WALKED IN SMELLING LIKE BEER AND UNWASHED pussy. But Tatiana knew better than to ask him where he'd been or with whom. He'd only lie, or worse yet, he might hit her. Her husband was still a handsome man. He had the square jaw, dark, smoldering eyes, tan skin, and lean, muscular build of a swimsuit model. But he was mean when he drank, and only a little less so when he was sober.

Levi was the descendent of Irish and Sicilian immigrants who had represented two separate gangs in Philadelphia. His mother and father were sort of a Romeo and Juliette story without the romantic ending. Instead, his parent's romance ended in seven kids, welfare checks, food stamps, and meth addiction. It was a miracle Levi wasn't even more fucked up than he was.

"Tatiana! Tatty, where you at?"

"I'm sleeping. It's one a.m., Levi!" Tatiana called out from her bedroom upstairs.

"I don't give a damn what time it is! Whose car is that outside?"

"What car?" Tatiana asked.

"There's a black car with tinted windows parked across the street. Who you got in here with you?"

"There's no one here, Levi. I'm just trying to sleep. Where have you been?"

"You don't fucking worry about where I been! I don't answer to you. I'm the man of this house!"

Tatiana heard her husband begin stomping angrily up the stairs, mumbling to himself. She knew he was going to hurt her. Quickly, she climbed out of bed and ran into the bathroom. She locked the door and climbed into the tub. He would kick down the door, like he always did, but she wasn't about to make it easy for him to get to her. They'd replaced enough doors over the past two years to replace every door in the seven thousand square foot house. Maybe, if he was drunk enough, he'd give up and fall asleep before he got to her. She could only hope. If he broke this door, the next one would be steel reinforced and come with a deadbolt.

Levi's footsteps halted.

"What the fuck? Who the hell – ? Get off of me!"

Then she heard a series of loud thumps and bumps, like someone falling, or being dragged, down the stairs. Tatiana was tempted to check on her husband, but if he was being attacked, if someone was here in the house, she was safer where she was. Besides, it was far more likely that Levi had simply fallen down the stairs.

Several minutes went by. Tatiana strained to hear what was going on downstairs. She'd heard a few more soft thumps, but then nothing. The silence was threatening. It was like the house had closed itself off and was keeping secrets from her. Keeping her from knowing what was happening to Levi. Conspiring to make her leave the fragile safety of her locked bathroom.

"Levi?"

Fight For Me

147

The silence remained like a sentinel, guarding her from whatever awfulness had transpired below.

"It's probably nothing," Tatiana assured herself. The sound of her own voice echoing off the marble shower tiles and floor in the dark bathroom was worse than the silence. She thought about calling her father, but she'd left her phone by the bed, and she couldn't let her dad know that he'd been right about Levi. She had no choice but to go downstairs and check on him.

Tatiana climbed out of the six-foot long, freestanding tub and reached for the bathrobe that always hung from the hook behind the door. She put the robe on over her nightgown and cinched the belt tight, then unlocked the door. Levi's guns were in a locked safe in the closet, but he had never trusted her with the combination, so she was weaponless as she crept slowly down the stairs, trying her best not to make a sound. She heard voices down there, so she paused. Frozen on the stairs. There were people in the house. People here to hurt Levi, and possibly her too.

Someone screamed, shrieked. The sound sent chills, like tendrils of cold fire, shooting up her spine, raising goosebumps all over her skin and weakening her knees. It sounded like Levi. Not really. He'd never made a sound like that before. But who else could it be? Unless he'd somehow gotten the better of his attackers in his inebriated state, which was unlikely, it had to be Levi. Whatever they were doing to him, they weren't being quick about it. They were taking their time, making him suffer. Tatiana imagined what she would tell his drunken, methhead, mother when she asked if her son had suffered. She knew the question would bring back the memory of that agonized wail, and the woman would see it all over her face, if she wasn't high at the time.

"Oh, my God. Jesus Christ!"

It was a woman's voice. She was whispering, but Tatiana was certain it was the voice of a woman, a woman who was horrified by whatever was happening to Levi. The anguished screams had stopped, replaced by moaning, and a gurgling, wheezing sound. In her heart, she knew it was Levi, and that she was listening to the last sounds he would ever make.

Tatiana wasn't sure she still loved Levi. He was an asshole. He was abusive, lazy, and unfaithful, but she had loved him once, and he could still be sweet sometimes. One thing she was absolutely certain of, she did not love him enough to go down those stairs and try to save him. Besides, he wasn't making noises anymore. He was probably beyond saving. If she crept back upstairs, she could lock herself in the bathroom again. This time, she would remember to grab her cell phone. If she called for help, maybe the cops would get there before whoever was hurting Levi could hurt her too.

She took a backwards step. Then another, and another. She was almost at the top of the stairs, preparing to turn and head back to her bedroom, when she heard the sound of footsteps heading away from her, slow, unhurried footsteps, then the "beep, beep, click" of the backdoor opening and closing. The alarm that they never set when they were home alerting them that a door had been opened. *Maybe they left?* Tatiana thought. But she wasn't sure. Definitely not certain enough to go down there and check. She decided to stick to her plan.

Quietly, Tatiana managed to tip-toe back to her bedroom, lock the door, and find her cell phone. She was just about to barricade herself in the bathroom when she remembered what Levi had said about a car parked across the street. She went to the window and looked out just as a black sedan pulled away from the curb and drove off down the block. It was too dark and too far away for her to see the license plate or even identify the make of the vehicle. It didn't matter to her, really. All that mattered was they were gone. She let out a sigh of relief and began dialing the police.

"Nine-one-one dispatch, what is your emergency."

"I think someone broke into my house. I think my husband might be hurt. I think he's dead."

"Are they still in the house? Are you somewhere safe?"

"I – I don't know. I think they left. I saw a car drive away, and I don't hear anyone anymore."

"Okay. We are sending units right away. Are you injured?"

"I'm okay. I was upstairs. They never came upstairs. But – my husband – I don't think he's okay."

"What is your name, ma'am?"

"Tatiana. Tatiana Ottum. My husband's name is Levi." For not the first time, Tatiana wondered how she'd ever wound up with someone with a hillbilly, redneck name like Levi? His name alone should have been a red flag.

"Okay. Just stay where you are, Mrs. Ottum. Help is on the way."

"I think my husband needs help. I have to go help him."

"Ma'am, just stay where you are. Police and paramedics are on their way."

Tatiana understood that there was probably nothing she could do for her husband. It didn't sound like the intruders had come here just to hurt him. Whatever they had done to him had been enough to horrify one of them. It had been enough to make Levi scream like a cat on fire. It had been enough to stop Levi from making any more noise. That didn't sound like just roughing him up. It sounded final. Permanent. Tatiana was fighting with herself, with the guilt she felt for being slightly relieved by the prospect of Levi's demise. More than slightly relieved. Almost giddy.

"I have to go see," she said.

"Ma'am, you need to stay safe."

"I think they're gone. Maybe Levi's okay? Maybe I can help him?"

But that's not what she really wanted to do. She wanted proof of death. She wanted confirmation that her own personal nightmare was over, that the boogeyman was dead.

The operator continued to implore her to wait as Tatiana crept slowly down the stairs.

"Levi? Levi, are you okay?"

There was no response. Tatiana reached the bottom of the stairs and could see blood seeping from the family room into the entry hallway. She'd always told Levi that the floors were unlevel, and he'd insisted she was crazy, not wanting to admit that the "deal" he'd gotten on labor to install the ridiculously expensive, twenty-four inch by twenty-four inch, Italian travertine tile he'd picked out wasn't such a deal after all, and they should have gone with a more reputable company, even if they'd charged twice as much. Now, his blood following the slant of the floor and running toward the front door proved that she was right. They'd gotten ripped off on the install. If Levi was really dead, the first thing she was going to do was have all the floors redone, and done right.

"Levi?"

She walked into the living room and saw Levi's body immediately. It was everywhere. She knew why the woman had been so horrified.

Fight For Me 151

"Ma'am? Ma'am? Are you still there? The police are right outside your door."

"They – they ripped him apart."

"Excuse me? I can't hear you."

The doorbell rang, and a heavy fist pounded on the door.

"SFPD! Open up!"

"They tore him apart. There's pieces of him all over the living room. They tore him apart!"

The door busted in and two officers stormed into the hall, then followed the river of blood into the family room. If they had been just a few seconds sooner, one of them might have caught her before Tatiana fainted and collapsed, striking her head on the improperly laid, unlevel, travertine marble floor.

20

KNOWING THE DEPTH OF VIOLENCE AND DEPRAVITY MY Master was capable of and actually seeing it with my own eyes were two entirely separate things I discovered when I watched him pull that man's intestines out through the opening he'd made from the man's pelvis to beneath his chin while the man was still relatively conscious and aware and screaming for his life. Tyrell had continued to reach inside him and rip out organs, tossing them around the room in a frenzy. Then, he'd begun sawing on him, severing limbs and other appendages before finally removing the man's head. I wanted to participate. I'd wanted to show my Master that I had the stomach for this, but I didn't. I could do a clean kill, a bullet through the head, even slitting someone's throat or stabbing them in the heart. I was prepared for that. Master had prepared me well to take a life without thinking. He hadn't prepared me for this.

Tyrell breathed heavily beside me as we drove away. He wasn't nervous. I knew better than that. He was excited. Sexually aroused. After two months together, I recognized the symptoms. As if to confirm this, he unzipped his pants and pulled out his cock.

"Master, I don't think I can right now. I feel – "

He didn't let me finish the sentence, grabbing me by the back of the neck and forcing my head down onto his engorged cock. All the work I'd done to rid myself of my gag reflex had to be employed when I felt his hand, still wet with that man's blood, still reeking of his intestines, of death, on the back of my neck. When the nausea I'd been feeling ever since I saw my Master tear out the man's lungs and toss them onto the couch began to stir the bile in my stomach at the same time as my Master's cock slid past my tonsils. There was no sense arguing with him, so I did as commanded and sucked my Master's cock as he drove us away from a murder.

"Take off your dress," Tyrell said, and I lifted my head off his cock to make sure I'd heard his command correctly.

"Sorry, Master? Did you say?" I didn't get the words out before my Master grabbed the front of my dress and ripped it completely off of me. We were on the freeway now, doing eighty, and he never took his eyes off the road.

"Sit on my cock."

This time, I didn't argue or protest. I climbed onto his lap, eased his cock inside me, and began to ride him. In no time at all, my nausea was gone, replaced by the ecstasy of my Master's lips on mine, his left hand cupping my ass and lifting me up and down, his cock thrusting up inside me, his mouth leaving mine to suckle my breasts before returning his eyes to the road. By the time we took the exit onto the freeway that would take us back to the house, I was on my third orgasm. Then the phone rang. My phone.

For the first month I was gone, my phone rang all the time. Annoyed with it, Master had taken it away. He'd only given it back a week ago. I'd listened to all my messages and read over eighty text messages from people wondering where the hell I'd disappeared to. I learned that Master had almost been right about the length of time it had taken for the salon to give my seat to someone else. Five weeks. He'd been off by a week. There were a few messages on there from Becca, updating me on Trish. Trish had taken over my apartment and seemed to be doing well. She'd told Becca that she wasn't seeing Manuel anymore, hadn't even heard from him, but Becca was suspicious. Becca was suspicious of everyone, though.

There were a couple messages from Dillon letting me know that he was all healed up and was training again. He said the gym had closed down and David had disappeared, and wanted to know if I knew anything about it and what had happened that night after he went to the hospital. Master had bought the gym, and we went there to train occasionally. I suspected, though he'd never admit it, that it held sentimental value for him. Dillon left me the address and phone number of the gym he was training at now and invited me to come train with him. That would never happen.

The texts and phone calls had gradually petered out, until it was only robocalls from people reminding me that my car's warranty was about to expire and companies trying to sell me healthcare. So, when the phone kept ringing and ringing, someone hanging up and calling back three times in a row, I finally asked Master for permission to answer it.

"Not yet," he said, then began strangling me with one hand while still driving with the other, and pistoning up inside me. I came again. I always had the most powerful orgasms when he was choking me, and this time was no different. I hit my head on the car ceiling as I tossed my head back and arched my back, feeling waves of pleasure buffet me like the ovean against the shore. Master came too. The car swerved a little as he emptied himself inside me, but he quickly regained control. I climbed off of his lap, picked up my phone, and looked at him.

"Clean me up first," he said, and I knew he didn't mean with a wet napkin. I bent over and licked his semen and my own juices from his still erect cock. I couldn't wait for us to get home so I could ride him again, and maybe even sit on his face. For such a dominant man, he loved it when I sat on his face and ground my labia against his lips. It was one of his favorite positions.

I licked the last of his seed from his pubic hair, and Master nodded his approval.

"Go ahead and answer your phone."

My smile lasted right up until I heard the voice message from Becca.

"Trish is dead," I said, repeating the message to my Master. Then I began to bawl, sobbing my eyes out. Trish was dead. Manuel had murdered her, and it was my fault. I should have been there to protect her.

Master pulled the car over to the shoulder, and pulled me into his lap, cradling me in his arms like an infant. He didn't say a word, just let me cry.

"That piece of shit killed her! That fucking piece of shit killed Trish!"

"What do you want me to do?" Master asked.

"I want to find Manuel."

"And?"

"I want to make him suffer. I want to kill him, and I want it to be messy."

"Are you sure?"

"Yes, Sir. I've never been more sure about anything."

Fight For Me   157

"Can you find out where he is?"

"He's at the police station. The police are questioning him, but Becca said they were going to let him go. They don't have enough evidence to charge him yet."

"That's good then. Which police station?"

"I -I don't know. I assume the precinct by my house. But, Becca didn't say."

"Can Becca be trusted?"

"What do you mean?"

"Can you call her back and ask her what precinct Manuel is at, without her telling the police you asked when his body is found?"

"Becca wouldn't say anything. She almost killed him once herself."

Tyrell nodded.

"Then call her back."

My hands trembled as I pulled up Becca's number in my contacts and hit the dial button.

"Becca?"

"Did you get my message?"

"Where is he?"

"He's at the police station. They're questioning him, but I talked to the detective in charge of the case, and he said they didn't have enough evidence to hold him. They are trying to get a warrant to search his place, but he already called a lawyer. A fucking lawyer. How did that piece of shit get a lawyer? He must have called one right after he killed her and had him standing by. Maybe he even talked to a lawyer before he killed her, to get his fucking alibi straight."

"Which precinct is he at?"

"The fifteenth. Right by Manuel's house."

"We're on our way."

"We?"

"Me – me and my – my Master."

"Your what? You mean the guy that fucked up Dillon?"

"He can help."

There was a long pause.

"I'll meet you there."

"No, Becca. You don't want to be involved in all of this."

"What the fuck are you talking about? Trish was my friend too. Fuck that! I'm on my way. I'm going to kill that motherfucker."

"Okay. Okay. We'll be there in twenty minutes."

"What did she say?" Master asked.

"She's coming too. She wants to help."

Tyrell stared bullet holes through my skull, then slowly shook his head.

"She can't come. Call her back."

"She won't take no for an answer, Sir."

"And I don't leave witnesses. So, it's your choice how this night ends."

In the two months we'd been together, I'd never once defied Tyrell's will. I'd never argued. Never disputed his word. But, not this time.

"Then we'll do it without you. Just let me out," I said, scrambling out of his lap, back into my seat and pulling on the door handle. Master engaged the child safety locks.

"No. You're mine."

"Let me out!" I yelled, pulling harder on the door handle.

"No," he said without the slightest hint of emotion.

"Trish was my friend! She doesn't mean shit to you. You don't have to do this, but I do! And, Becca does. You showed me everything I need to know. I won't get caught," I said between sobs. I knew I sounded hysterical. Tears streamed

Fight For Me 159

from my eyes, and my nose had begun to run. I felt like a child throwing a tantrum.

"Yes, you will. Because this isn't some random stranger. This is the guy who killed your friend. You'll be emotional, sloppy. You'll leave evidence. You'll be questioned, and you'll crack, or Becca will."

"You don't know Becca."

"I know you."

I stood my ground, raising my chin to meet his gaze.

"No. You only know part of me. A small part."

Master seized me by the throat. I flinched, but didn't look away. I wasn't going to give up on this.

"I know that you almost threw up seeing what I did to that meal tonight. I know you were thinking about quitting, leaving me, because it was too much for you."

"I – I ..."

"Don't deny it. I know it crossed your mind. But now, because it's personal, someone you think deserves to die, you suddenly think you have the balls for this? Let me tell you something, Athena, that guy I destroyed tonight, he deserved to die. He was no better than this Manuel guy. He would have eventually killed his wife too."

I jerked my neck from his grip, but took my hand off the door handle and crossed my arms across my chest, staring straight ahead, fully aware that I still looked like a pouting child.

"I wouldn't have left you."

"But you thought about it. For a moment, you considered it."

My bottom lip quivered and more tears came.

"It was just so – so brutal, Sir. It was – it was like something from a horror movie."

Master smiled, then shook his head slowly.

"And yet, I've done so much worse. I will do worse. We'll do worse tonight. Can you handle that?"

"Yes."

"Can Becca?"

I thought about it. I thought about the hatred and fury Becca had shown when she had Manuel at her mercy. There was no doubt in my mind.

"Yes. She can."

Master released his grip on my throat and leaned back in his seat.

"Because, if she can't, you know what I'll have to do?"

"I know. It'll be okay."

21

FUCKING PIGS, MANUEL THOUGHT. *MAKING ALL THIS DAMN FUSS over some dead whore. They didn't know her. They don't know what she did to me.*

He hadn't meant to kill her, but she definitely deserved it. She was the one who sent those fucking bitches to his place to fuck him up and – and – humiliate him. That bitch deserved everything she got. He would miss her. She was a great piece of ass, and she had always taken good care of him, cooking meals for him, paying his bills, buying him shit. But she shouldn't have sent those bitches to fuck with him.

He'd been sure to get rid of his clothes. He knew from watching detective shows on TV that the police could track his whereabouts through the GPS in his cellphone, so he'd left it at home whenever he followed Trish. He'd left his cell phone at home the day he followed her back to that big bitch's apartment where Trish had been staying. Manuel had taken the fire escape up to the roof, broke into the building through the exit door on the roof, then made sure he had his hood up and all the cameras were at his back as he made his way down the stairs to the floor where Trish was staying. He'd learned that from a detective show too. That's why he had to get rid of the clothes. When they checked the security cameras, the cops would see what clothes and shoes he was wearing. Besides, there was blood all over them.

"Go away, Manuel!" Trish said, when he knocked on the door. Fuck that! He'd kicked open the door, just like they did on those detective shows. The door struck her as it flew open.

"Get out of here, Manuel! I'm calling the police!" She'd kept saying his name, hoping the neighbors heard it. But he'd been smart about that too. It was mid-day. All her neighbors were at work. Their kids were in school. There was no one to hear her scream. No one to call the police. If she'd gotten a fucking job, instead of hiding herself away in that big bitch's apartment for weeks, maybe she wouldn't have been home either. Maybe she'd still be alive.

"Fucking bitch!" he yelled when he landed the first punch that drove the back of her head into the hardwood floor and made her eyes roll up in her head.

"Fucking whore!" He said, when he punched her again, and again, and again, and again.

"Slut!"

"Dyke bitch!"

He hadn't meant to kill her, but he knew he might if he kept punching her like that. He remembers seeing her body start to convulse, and thinking to himself that he should probably stop hitting her in the face. But he hadn't stopped. He'd kept hitting her harder, and harder, and harder, until her face was unrecognizable. Until her eyes were swollen shut, and there were gashes above and below each eyelid, her nose was smashed flat, lips ripped open, and then, he'd

Fight For Me 163

begun to strangle her. He was sure she was already dead by that point, but he had done it anyway. He couldn't stop himself. It wasn't his fault. She had made him crazy. That didn't sound like a great defense. So, he'd cleaned up the scene, wiping away his fingerprints and shoe prints and any trace of himself that he could think to get rid of. He'd even vacuumed her clothes to remove any hair or clothing fibers. He'd seen that on a cop show too.

He'd tied his clothes and shoes up in a bundle and driven out to the bridge overlooking the bay, but there were too many cameras on the bridge because of all the people who used it to commit suicide or dispose of bodies. So, he'd kept driving. He drove all the way into the Marin headlands, into the redwood forest, and walked for over an hour. He buried his clothes as deep in the forest as he could think to go, covered the freshly turned dirt with leaves and branches, then assessed the area to see if anyone would notice it if they didn't know it was there. Nope. He'd done good.

On the way back into the city, he stopped at a Salvation Army and bought new clothes and shoes, then donated the clothes he'd worn out into the woods, including another pair of shoes. Killing that bitch had been expensive. But minutes after he'd gotten home, two detectives came knocking at his door to question him about his whereabouts. Luckily, he'd stopped at El Toro on his way home and bought a burrito. He held it up by way of reply.

"I was hungry."

They asked him if they could search his apartment, and he obliged them. Then they asked him when the last time he'd seen Trish.

"She left me two months ago."

"And you haven't seen her since?"

"Nope. She won't even return my calls." He knew they'd

check her cell phone records, like they did on his favorite detective show. They'd see that he'd called her many times, but he hadn't spoken to her in over two months. He'd stopped calling her a week ago. Once he knew where she was, there'd been no need to keep calling.

The detectives asked him if he'd been wearing the same clothes all day. He told them he had. He'd paid for them in cash and removed the tags and threw them away right there in the store, and he never kept receipts. They would have no way of knowing he'd just bought those clothes. They told them to take them off and put them in a bag. He went into the bathroom and took off the clothes, smiling the entire time.

They had taken him down to the station and kept him there for two hours. He'd insisted on calling his cousin's lawyer before leaving the apartment. Since he was going voluntarily, and wasn't actually under arrest, they couldn't really stop him from making a call. And once they knew he'd called a lawyer, they couldn't really question him until his lawyer showed up, not unless he started volunteering information, which he wasn't going to do.

Manuel's cousin sold drugs. Lots of drugs. His lawyer was pretty good. Manuel walked out of the police station without ever saying a single word to the detectives. Now, he was back home, having a beer, deciding if it would make sense for him to go after those two bitches who hurt him, or if hurting Trish had been enough. They'd know Trish's death was their fault, and it would kill them that Manuel had gotten away with it, and he was sure he would.

Someone knocked on his door, and Manuel rolled his eyes and let out a sigh. He knew it was either the detectives again, here to ask him more questions, try to catch him without his lawyer. He knew their games. He'd seen them do that on detective shows. Or, it was those bitches, here to get revenge. They'd caught him by surprise last time, but this time he would be ready. He had a baseball bat by the door, and he looked forward to bashing their fucking heads in with it.

Manuel walked to the door and looked out. There was a huge black guy with long, neat, perfectly symmetrical, salt and pepper dreadlocks. He wore a black suit, black shirt, and black tie, and his eyes were as green as emeralds, despite his blueish black skin.

"Who is it?"

"Manuel Ortiz? I'm Detective Lozano. I have a few more questions for you that we forgot to ask down at the station."

Manuel rolled his eyes and unlocked the door.

"I need to call my lawyer again. I'm not saying shit without my – "

His words were cut off by a punch to his throat, followed by one to his solar plexus. He dropped to his knees, and the big black guy pushed past him, followed by those two bitches. Manuel tried to get his throat to work so he could scream for help before his apartment door closed and he was stuck in here alone with the big guy and those crazy bitches, but he couldn't catch his breath. He watched in horror as the little one, Becca, closed his apartment door, then knelt down beside him, showing him the switchblade knife with a leopard on the handle and the brass knuckles she was carrying.

"You should have left her alone like we told you to. You fucked up, Manuel."

Yup. He'd definitely fucked up. He knew how this was going to end. With him tied to a chair with duct tape over his mouth, getting beaten and tortured, just like he'd seen on those detective shows.

22

"ARE SURE YOU'RE BOTH UP FOR THIS?" MY MASTER ASKED FOR about the sixth or seventh time since we picked Becca up from her apartment.

Becca answered by punching Manuel in the side with her brass knuckles, then doubling it up to the head with a left hook. I didn't want to punch him. I wanted to cut him.

"Don't knock him out. I want him awake for this. For all of this," I said.

"I need to hear you say it," Master insisted.

"We're up for it. Ain't nobody pussying out," Becca replied. There was a coldness in her voice that obviously connected with Tyrell. He nodded, and Becca landed two more punches to Manuel's ribs with her brass knuckles.

I pulled out the tanto knife, a gift from Master, and stabbed Manuel in the thigh. He screamed, but the sound was muffled by the sock in his mouth and the duct tape wrapped around his lips. I twisted the knife around in his leg before pulling it out. Master sat down on the couch to watch. He was clearly enjoying this.

"Let's cut his balls off," Becca said.

I had been thinking the same thing. Unfortunately, we'd already taped his legs to the chair, so getting his pants off would be hard. Master, of course, had a solution.

"Here. Just cut his pants off of him," Master said, handing me his pearl-handled straight razor. Manuel screamed even louder then. The chords in his neck and the veins in his temples bulged and throbbed with the effort, but the gag kept the sound to a minimum.

I cut from his knee, up one thigh, across his crotch, and down the other thigh to the opposite knee, then peeled back his jeans in one big flap. Manuel squirmed and thrashed the entire time. Cutting his boxer briefs off was quicker. I nicked the head of his cock in the process. Manuel's entire body tensed up and shook in pain and terror. His cock shriveled and retreated like a snake slithering back into its den. Urine and blood dribbled from two separate openings in the head of his cock. The nick had been unintentional, but the second, third, and fourth cuts I made in the head of his cock, butterflying it into a fan of bleeding flesh, were completely deliberate. I wished I could have heard his screams.

"Jesus, Athena," Becca said, watching me filet Manuel's manhood.

I wasn't done yet. I cut open his scrotum and pulled out his testicles. They dangled from that wrinkled, bleeding sack on thin, winding chords. I caught them and crushed them in my palm one at a time like grapes. I looked over at my Master, half-expecting him to be wincing and squeezing his knees together the way most men would upon seeing another man emasculated in this way, but his face remained stoic. Except his eyes. There was hunger and madness in his eyes.

Becca shook her head.

Fight For Me   169

"I think that's enough," she said. That's when Master stood and walked over to us, to Manuel.

"You can leave if you don't want to see this," Master said.

"Maybe – maybe you should leave. It's okay. We'll take care of this."

I could see the indecision on Becca's face. I know she wanted to support me, to avenge Trish, but she was having difficulty stomaching this level of brutality.

Becca looked from my face to my Master's to Manuel's. Then she stepped forward, took the knife from my hands, and shoved it Manuel's eye socket, pushing it in deep until she hit brain. She watched his body thrash and convulse for a few seconds while blood poured from his eye socket like an open faucet. Then, she turned her back on him, on me and Tyrell, and walked out of the apartment.

"Is she going to be okay?" Master asked. His question was not based in concern for her well-being, but for her silence.

I nodded. "She will be. She just needs time."

"I'll call the cleaners," Master said, retrieving his cell phone.

They showed up in thirty minutes, the same crew that had disposed of David's body. We stood there watching them work for a few minutes, but when they took out the hacksaws and axes, I let Master know that I was ready to go.

"You're going to need to drive."

"Why, Sir? My license is expired."

"Still, you're white. It'll be better than me driving."

"I – I don't know if I can. I'm still shaking," I confessed, more than slightly embarrassed.

"Never mind," Master said.

We had driven only six blocks when red and blue lights

flashed in the rearview mirror. Master looked at me with undisguised fury. I should have driven.

"Shit."

Master let out a long sigh as he pulled over to the curb. I knew he still had his guns on him, in the shoulder holster under his sports jacket. And Master was right, him being a black man increased the chances of our car being searched. I hadn't considered how much everyday racism could make it harder to be a contract killer.

The cop sat in his vehicle for a few minutes, no doubt running our plates. Then he got out of his cruiser and began walking toward the car on the passenger side.

"Here. Take my phone. Byrd's number is in there. Call him and tell him we are going to need new identities and a new car. "

I took the phone and began dialing, just as the police officer reached our car and shined a flashlight in the backseat, and then into our faces. He gestured for me to roll down the window. Byrd answered the phone.

"Ty?"

"This is Athena. Tyrell told me to call. He said we need new Ids and a new vehicle."

"Why?"

Two shots rang out, deafening me. The police officer dropped to the pavement with two holes in his chest. Tyrell got out, and walked around the front of the car with his back turned, presumably to avoid the police cruiser's dash camera. Then he stepped around and put two more bullets in the officer's skull.

"Because he just killed a cop," I said.

"Oh. Where do you want me to send it?"

I gave him our address, surprised that he didn't already have it. Master opened my car door.

Fight For Me 171

"Now, you drive."

This time, I didn't argue.

We didn't relax until we were safely out of the city.

"Where is Byrd sending our new identification?"

"To our house."

"What?"

His tone had changed. He stared at me for a long moment, as if deciding whether or not to bash my face into the dashboard until I stopped breathing. At least, that's how I interpreted his expression. He wasn't happy.

"He – he's sending it all to our house."

"You gave him our address?"

"Y-yes."

Master turned back to focus on the road.

"That isn't good."

That was all he said for the rest of the drive.

23

WE WENT BACK HOME, BACK TO OUR LIFE OF ISOLATION, training, and discipline. I was spending six to eight hours a day becoming a better killer, improving my striking and grappling, learning to shoot, learning knife techniques and torture techniques.

"What about explosives?" I asked.

Master chuckled.

"I am not a jack of all trades. There are guys who specialize in that sort of thing. My specialty is up close and personal."

"So, I guess no sniper rifles either?"

"Too impersonal."

"Doesn't getting close put you at greater risk?"

Master smiled.

"It wouldn't be as much fun without the risk. I want to see the fear and pain on their faces when they go."

Fun. It was fun for him. I knew this. I had known it since the tournament. When he murdered David, pulverized his skull with elbows, it was fun. When he gutted that wife-beater, tore him apart and scattered his meat and organs around the room like confetti, it had been fun. All of this was fun for him. He wanted to "see the fear and pain on their faces." It wasn't just a job. They say, find a job you love and you'll never work a day in your life. Tyrell loved killing. And, the truth was, I was beginning to enjoy it too.

It had been less than a week since Master's last meal, the wife-beater, less than a week since we'd avenged Trish's murder. We had a new car, new drivers' licenses, and new passports. We hadn't heard from Byrd, but that was normal. Master didn't work every day. This town would be littered with eviscerated corpses if he did. But I was worried, because I could tell Master was worried.

There were suddenly more guns and rifles around, strategically placed in every room of the house. There were four guns in the living room alone, three more in the dining room, and at least that many in the kitchen. There wasn't a room in the house where a firearm was not within arm's reach.

I finally worked up the nerve to ask what was on his mind.

"Is someone coming for us, Master? Is Byrd going to send someone after us? Are we still safe here?"

Master stared at me in that uncomfortable, intense way he had. Not like he was undressing you with his eyes, but like he was dissecting you.

"I don't know," he finally said.

"Should we leave? Find somewhere else?"

"I like it here," Master said. I didn't press the issue, and I didn't bring it up again, but I could tell Master was anxious. Then, on the sixth day after the murders, the phone rang.

"The wife saw you."

"No one saw us."

"Well, she saw something. She's hired a private investigator to track you down."

"We didn't leave any evidence. He won't find us."

"Why are you still in that town?"

"Because I like it here."

"It's making the client nervous. He's afraid that investigator is going to find you."

"It would be bad for him if he did. Very bad."

"That's not the point. The client is worried about his daughter finding out that he ordered the hit."

"She'd probably thank him."

"These domestic things are tricky. He's worried his daughter might still have loved that asshole. That maybe she didn't want him dead, and she'll hate him if she finds out her father had her husband killed."

"Like I said, I was careful. That investigator won't find anything, and if he did, he'd get dealt with."

"But –"

"If he's this paranoid, perhaps he wasn't properly vetted. Maybe he's a liability. Maybe you both are?"

"It's not that simple. You can't just kill this guy. He's powerful. Real powerful. He has connections that go all the way to the White House. How do you think that clown in the oval office got elected? He cannot risk a scandal."

"Then reassure him, Byrd. Otherwise, I will be forced to take other measures."

"Okay, okay, I'll talk to him."

"And, Byrd ... next time you call, have a job for me."

Tyrell didn't talk to me about the call. I'd heard it all, and it sounded serious, but I knew better than to pry. If he felt it was something I should know, he would tell me, and I just had to accept that. This was his world, and my obedience was the price for being a part of it. I just wasn't certain how long I could continue playing this submissive role. I mean, I loved being dominated. Having a man who could so thoroughly control me sparked something deep within me. Master had called it my "slave heart."

"Human beings, as social animals, crave these hierarchical structures. It's how governments and kingdoms came to be. From sports to business to our romantic relationships, we have a desire to lead or be led. In most relationships, vanilla relationships, where there is no clear leader, there are power struggles. Each person battling for control, resisting their partner's attempts to wield power. We call those relationships egalitarian, but in practice they are often anarchy, chaos, and lead to them both hating each other. However, when one of them accepts the natural dominance and leadership abilities of the other, and willfully accepts the submissive role, there is no strife, no battle. There is harmony. Ideally. But, as social animals, it is also normal for leadership roles to change. The dominant partner, if he or she wishes to remain so, must continually reassert their dominance, or risk being dethroned."

"Do you think I would dethrone you?"

Master smiled.

"I think you would try." He looked at me with an expression of honest appreciation and pride. "And, someday, you would succeed."

I thought about what it would look like with our roles reversed, me as the Master, and Tyrell as my slave. I didn't like it.

"No. My submission is my gift to you. I don't ever want it back."

"You are wrong. Submission should never be a gift. It is a reward. It is to be earned, not given away like charity. It would be worthless otherwise. I desired your submission

Fight For Me 177

because you made me literally fight for it, and I will fight every day to keep it."

I can't remember ever being wetter than I was hearing those words from him.

My life before the blood and death and violence, before my submission to Tyrell, felt like a fantasy that never was. The salon. My old apartment. Even Becca. It all felt like the vestiges of a dream that I had awakened from. Today, Master wanted me to fight him.

I was much stronger than I had been when I met Tyrell. He'd taught me so much, and my strength had increased dramatically from training with him. I could bench two hundred and twenty-five pounds, curl eighty-five pounds, and squat three hundred and fifteen pounds. I could run eight miles, spar fifteen rounds, and wrestle for hours. There weren't many men who would have been a match for me now, but the prospect of fighting Master still sent a tremble through my legs. Because he seemed to be getting stronger too.

Master boiled my new mouthpiece, and I bit down on it and formed it to my mouth. He wrapped my hands and put on a pair of MMA gloves that were still stiff and new. Those were all I was allowed to wear.

"Um, no clothes?"

"No."

Master took off his pants and underwear. His semi-erect cock hung like a pendulum between his legs. I guess we were going to fight naked. I wondered what he would do if a grabbed his balls, or punched him in the dick? It was probably best not to find out. Or, perhaps I would save those as a last resort.

"Master?"

"Yes?"

"Why have you been training me so hard? What if I get so good that I can beat you?"

Master looked at me with a smile playing at the corners of his mouth. The look in his eyes was both loving and amused.

"Only weak men desire weak women. Your submission is valuable to me because you are strong, the strongest woman I have ever met. And the stronger you get, the more valuable you are to me. It is not a question of if you will someday surpass me. It's just a question of when. I am older than you, and not getting younger."

His answer opened up so many more questions, but they were questions for another day, another time.

We walked out into the field, onto the gun range, and squared off. Master took a traditional upright Muay Thai stance, fists raised, chin lowered, knees shoulder width apart and slightly bent, up on the balls of his feet. I chose a lower, wrestler's stance, but I kept my hands up high.

"Begin," Master said, and I froze, just for a second, but long enough for him to land a kick to my thigh that made my legs buckle. His shin cut into my thigh like an ax blade. It felt like he'd chopped through the muscle and fat and hit bone. I half expected to see blood, my leg lopped off and only a bleeding stumo remaining. Pain shot like a jolt of electricity up and down my leg. I'd been kicked many times in training, but I had never been kicked like that. I didn't go down, though. Instead, I returned Master's leg kick with one of my own to the outside of his lead leg, then followed it with a kick to his inside thigh. Master smiled. He was impressed. He also wasn't taking me seriously. I decided to use that to my advantage and threw another kick, this one to his head.

I knew the kick wouldn't land. Master leaned back,

Fight For Me 179

easily avoiding the blow. My kick sailed harmlessly past his nose, missing by inches. But, in dodging the kick, he'd left his own leg exposed. I shot in for a single-leg take down, biting down on my mouthpiece, expecting to feel Master's knee bounce off my chin at any minute, but I had surprised him. I scooped his left leg up and drove my shoulder into his thigh, whipping his body to the left, trying to take him off balance. Master pushed down on my head, then turned his knee so it was aimed at the ground before easily jerking his leg from my grasp. I hadn't gotten the take down, but I had done something he hadn't been expecting. I had to keep up the attack.

I threw a push kick to Master's stomach that he easily swatted aside. He deflected my attempt at a jab, cross, hook combination, then threw a straight knee to my solar plexus that doubled me over. I tried to suck in another breath, but the pain in my abdomen was so great that my lungs would not expand. I was helpless. Master drew back his right fist across his chest, up to his left ear, then backhanded me with it, knocking me to the floor. It was not the most powerful blow he could have landed in that moment. I knew he had taken it easy on me, but a back fist to the jaw felt almost disrespectful. It was how a man hits a woman, not how men hit men. At least, that's how I interpreted it, and it pissed me off. I rolled to my feet and charged at him, throwing a flurry of punches. A jab landed, he blocked the overhand right and my left hook, and then my uppercut landed, whipping his head back, then I kneed him in the balls.

I had not intended to do that. There were few circumstances under which I would have considered attacking Master's manhood an acceptable tactic, and a friendly sparring session was not one of them. Master buckled, but didn't drop. I cracked him with a slashing elbow to the temple, and this time he stumbled backwards. I was winning! Perhaps I had cheated. He had never actually established the rules. Perhaps I would be punished for this later. But right now, I was beating him. I felt a surge of adrenaline. I was ecstatic as I closed the distance, winding up a big right hook that I was certain would end the fight. I threw it with everything I had, but it was too wide. The shortest distance between two points is a straight line, and it was a straight right that crashed into my jaw like a sledgehammer and turned out my lights.

Master was inside me. I felt his cock filling me up, his urgent thrusting ripping the walls of my vagina, his teeth latched down on the back of my neck, biting through skin and drawing trickles of warm blood that dripped down between my shoulder blades. He growled in my ear. Deep, rumbling, savage sounds that vibrated through my entire body. I responded with a splash that lubricated his cock and made his thrusts less painful. I let out a moan. He responded with more vicious growls, more brutal thrusts, and a hand around my throat, pressing down on my carotid artery and trachea. I felt lightheaded, like I was going to blackout again, but I also felt an imminent orgasm. When it came, it was like an avalanche, one orgasm tumbling down into another, and another, each building in intensity. Then, everything went black. I wondered briefly if Master would continue fucking me if I died. And then chastised myself for such a silly notion.

Of course he would.

The bamboo sheets felt amazingly comfortable. I could vaguely remember Master lifting me in his arms, after knocking me unconscious, fucking me awake, then choking me unconscious again. I remember him putting an ice pack on my jaw for the swelling and giving me some ibuprofen,

Fight For Me 181

then carrying me up to bed. There was still daylight then. Now, the sun was long gone.

The house was silent. I listened for the familiar sound of the grandfather clock that had been in the dining room of my parent's house, but I hadn't lived with them in years, and Tyrell had no clocks. There was only the rustle of the wind through the trees off in the distance, and the deep, sonorous, rumble of Master's breaths as he slept beside me.

My jaw still hurt. I smiled, thinking to myself, *I almost had him*. Yes, he had taken me lightly, and that had allowed for some of the openings I took advantage of, but just two months ago, I would not even have been able to take advantage of those opportunities. In the last nine weeks with Tyrell, I had almost been through the equivalent of a full training camp, like I was training for the fight of my life. My skills had improved in leaps and bounds. I wondered when I would get a chance to test them. I thought about throwing a new tournament, only this time they would have to fight me. I loved the idea of it. It was like the first time I fought Dillon. I felt like I would have mopped the floor with Dillon now.

Footsteps.

I sat up in bed, listening. I heard them again. Stealthy footsteps creeping down the hall. No alarms had gone off. Master must have been so busy caring for me that he forgot to set the security alarm. I slipped out of bed and retrieved the Glock from its holster taped behind the headboard. I nudged Master twice before his eyes opened.

The only light in the room came from the moonlight pouring in through the four, small, three foot by three foot windows that were about two feet from the ceiling on the wall behind our bed, and the cellphone charger and open laptop screensaver, but it was enough. Master saw the pistol in my hand, aimed at the locked bedroom door, and I put a finger to his lips to silence him before he could ask any questions. It hadn't been necessary. He rolled out of bed and landed on both feet with hardly a sound, then crept over to the closet, returning with an M4A1 carbine, which he handed to me, taking my Glock and laying it down on the floor after gesturing for me to get out of the bed. He had chosen the big, heavy, AR-10 for himself, which fired 7.62 millimeter rounds instead of 5.56 millimeter rounds like the M4. Master had explained to me once on the gun range that some of the new body armor coming out of Russia could deflect 5.56 millimeter bullets, but not what the AR-10 spit.

We took up positions on opposite sides of the door, but angled toward the door like a triangle in order to avoid crossfire. Master was just a shadow standing across from me, but I could tell he was still naked, as was I. I wondered if we were both about to die, but I had faith in Master and how he had trained me. I had wanted a battle to test my skills. It seemed that I was about to get one. And, if I was going to die, falling in defense of my Master felt right. Us dying together felt right.

We listened. The footsteps were closer, so close that I could hear breathing on the other side of the door. Master crouched. Then gestured for me to do the same. Then he held up a fist. Hold. I was not to shoot until he told me to. The doorknob turned and the barrel of a gun peaked into the room. The positions we had chosen put the moonlight from the windows directly behind us, so the door, and whoever entered through it, were illuminated, but crouching down as we were, the light went over our heads, keeping us in shadow.

The door opened wider and a head peaked in, then ducked back, then stepped through. I hadn't received Master's signal yet. I held my breath so the man would not

Fight For Me 183

hear my breathing. I could hear his, though. It sounded like a freight train. He was scared. Of course he was. He must have known who Tyrell was. The door flew all the way open, and three more men stepped into our bedroom. That's when Master opened up with the AR-10, firing short three round bursts at each man, dropping them quickly and cleanly. I took aim at the man closest to me and was tempted to just hold down the trigger and emptied the entire thirty round magazine into him, but that was not how Master taught me. As the man swung his rifle toward Master, I fired three shots into his torso. The man dropped without firing a shot. In fact, I was pretty sure no one had fired a shot except us. Master reached under the bed and pulled out two heavy pieces of body armor.

"Put this on. There might be more of them. We need to clear the house."

"Why not just run down to the garage and drive out of here?"

"Because I don't have time to check for bombs."

That made terrifying sense. Master didn't like explosives, but who knew about whoever these guys were.

"Who are they?"

"Byrd sold us out. They probably work for the last client."

And I had given Byrd our address.

"I – I'm sorry, Sir."

Master nodded, acknowledging my apology, but not accepting it, or saying anything to relieve my guilt.

"Let's go."

We went from room to room, hugging the walls. We had just stepped out of one of the guest bedrooms when we saw the two men walk out of the kitchen. One was a handsome, square-jawed, Spanish guy, maybe Brazilian or Colombian, average height, with long, black hair, and a bulky, muscular physique, carrying a shotgun. The other had a short blond, buzz cut, a lean build, and was almost as tall as Tyrell. He carried an AR-15. He was the first to fire. Three bullets struck my Master in the chest. He staggered backward. I turned the M4 on the man and held down the trigger. Fuck saving ammo. I sprayed him with bullets until he was just featureless bleeding meat. In my peripheral vision, I saw the Spanish guy turn toward me with the shotgun. Then I saw him disappear, tackled to the floor and the shotgun wrenched from his grasp. Master straddled him, bashing his face in with the butt of his own shotgun. Brain and skull fragments spattered the kitchen walls.

Master stood. He was bleeding from a bullet that had gone through his forearm. Probably after the first two hit his torso, when he raised his arm instinctively in a defensive manner. The two bullets that had struck him in the chest hadn't pierced his body armor.

He stood and quietly surveyed the house. There was blood, bodies, and bullet holes everywhere.

"I'm calling the cleaners. This house is burned."

"Burned?"

"It means we can't live here anymore."

"Will you sell it?"

Master shook his head.

"When I say 'burned', I mean that literally. Let's go. I'll call on our way."

He took my hand and pulled me toward the garage.

"Where are we going?"

"To see the client."

"Master?"

"Yes?"

"Can you give me one more night? Just one last romantic

Fight For Me 185

night, before we go after this guy? Like when we went to the jazz club?"

Master paused and studied my face, a slight smile played at the corners of his mouth.

"Why?"

"In case this goes wrong. In case you die, or I die, or we both do. I just want us to have one good night first."

Master reached out and brushed a few stray hairs from my face, then cupped my cheek in his enormous palm. I snuggled against his hand. He smiled, and I thought I caught a shimmer of moisture in his eyes

"Okay. One night. But first, we need to gather up the guns and ammo. We might need all of it. Grab the night vision goggles also."

"Sounds like you're preparing for war."

Master nodded solemnly.

"We aren't coming back from this, are we?"

Master gathered me into his arms and gave me the first genuinely warm hug I could remember receiving from him. He kissed me on my forehead, then laid his head on top of mine.

"I promise I will protect you. You will survive this."

"But, what about you?"

Master shrugged. It felt like the world's most succinct suicide note.

24

THE NEW VEHICLE BYRD HAD PROVIDED US WITH WAS A SILVER Cadillac CTS-V four-door sedan. It had a turbo-charged 6.2L V8 640 horsepower engine that could go from zero to sixty in 30 seconds and reach a high speed of two hundred miles per hour. The perfect getaway car, should a fast escape become necessary, and odds were high that it would.

Master let me know that we would have to dump the new identities Byrd had provided for us after the cop killing as soon as the job was done. I was fine with that. I didn't really think I looked much like a Monica J. O'Rourke anyway.

"We can keep the car though, right?"

"We'll see. I'm more partial to Mercedes, but this isn't bad."

I drove us to a Brazilian steakhouse just outside the city, near the airport. This was a deliberate choice on my part to keep us away from the cops in the city. After killing that cop, our faces were all over the news, even if they had the wrong names to go with it and the license plate number and vehicle descriptions were to a car that had been set on fire and dumped into the ocean. Just dying my hair blonde and Master wearing a hat and sunglasses wasn't likely to fool anyone.

The steakhouse was perfect. Waiters darted to and from our table with various choice cuts of meat from filet mignon, prime rib, and New York strip, to pork chops, lamb chops, and bacon-wrapped chicken.

"I think I'm going to get some more salad."

I laughed.

"Sir, you don't go to a Brazilian steakhouse for the salad."

"Then I will buck the trend," Master replied.

"You rebel," I said, laughing. The waiter came by with the restaurant's signature dish called picanha, a prime cut of top sirloin marinated in garlic and other spices. I was already full, but I just couldn't resist. I asked for two, thin, medium rare slices.

"Well, I guess that means you won't have room for dessert," Master said as he ate his arugula and kale salad.

"I will make room if I have to turn this place into a Roman vomitorium."

Master didn't normally like crude jokes, but even he laughed at that one.

We were both stuffed by the time we rolled ourselves out of there. Master didn't drink alcohol, it dulls the senses, he said, so neither did I. Still, it was a wonderful meal.

"Where to now?"

"You wanted a date night, right? So, that means dinner and a show. We are going to the ballet. They are doing a co-production of Dracula along with the symphony. It's supposed to be spectacular."

I smiled. Somehow, I never pictured Master as a ballet type of guy, yet, somehow, it fit. Dracula definitely fit.

"Sounds wonderful."

Master draped an arm around my shoulders, and I snuggled tight against him as we walked to our car. He opened my car door, helped me inside, then closed my door before walking around to open his own. I could not stop smiling. This date was absolutely perfect, so far. I was still having a hard time relaxing, knowing that we both might be dead in the next twenty-four hours, but Master was helping me slowly let go and enjoy the moment.

The ballet was both beautiful and macabre. The symphony played dark ominous music as the dancers whirled and twirled in vampire costumes. Mad shadows cast against white curtains splashed with blood. It was thrilling in a way I had never imagined a ballet could be.

When we left the ballet, my heart was soaring. We held hands as we walked to our car, just like an ordinary couple. We smiled and laughed. Master opened my car door for me, then scooped me into his arms and kissed me passionately.

There was a question that had been troubling me ever since our sparring session. As I looked at my Master's handsome face, the face that made me feel safe, and for the first time in my life, small, I felt tiny in his massive arms, like a little lady.

"Will you always be my Master? I mean, what if you train me so well, if I get so good, that I beat you some day?"

Master laughed.

"Then that would depend on you. Is your submission to me conditional upon me being able to beat you in hand to hand combat? Or do you submit out of your inner need to serve, out of respect, and devotion? What about if I'm sick or injured? Will I no longer be your Master then? Is my authority over you conditional upon me being perfect, always making the right decisions? What about the job we just took? Am I no longer your Master because that went bad? Or am I your Master right or wrong, strong or weak? Is a king not still a king even when he makes a mistake?"

I didn't know the answer to that. I knew what I should say, what he wanted me to say, but I wasn't certain what was true in my heart. I certainly could never see Tyrell bowing before me. If I defeated him in battle, either nothing would change, or everything would end. I wasn't sure I ever wanted to know which of those possibilities were true. I did know one thing for certain, with everything in my heart.

"I love you, Master."

Intense moments create intense emotions. I knew the danger we were in had heightened our reaction to everything we were experiencing. The good food and amazing performance had done its part as well. Nothing we were feeling could be trusted. Still, at that moment, I truly loved him.

"I love you too, Athena," Master replied.

"Is the night over?"

Master nodded.

"It's time for our last meal of the evening."

25

"What's the point?" Andreyev asked. "I'm dying anyway. The chemo is just making me sick. Cancel my appointment. I want to die like a man."

Kazimir nodded.

"I will cancel it, sir."

"Cancel all of them."

"Yes, sir."

Kazimir had served Andreyev Krovopuskov and his family for twenty years. When Andreyev dies, he knew his service to the family would be over. Tatiana had never liked him. There was no way she would keep him around. But, until the old man died, Kazimir would continue to serve the Krovopuskov family faithfully.

"Have you heard from Mr. Byrd about our problem?"

"He says he is working on it."

"And the men we sent?"

"They're all dead, sir. Tyrell killed them all."

"One man?"

"One monster, sir. And his woman, I presume."

Andreyev took a deep breath of oxygen from the mask hanging around his neck.

"Tatiana must not know. We must find this man before she does. She's very resourceful."

"We will find them."

"I want all of our men out there looking for them."

"We don't have many left, sir. It isn't like the old days. You are an honest civilian now. We don't have an army of soldiers anymore. Just the few loyal ones, like me, who stayed. That is why we hired this man to begin with."

Andreyev nodded. His face looked solemn and tired, but not defeated. His was a face that had witnessed the fall of communism and the rise of Russian capitalism, and, with it, Russian crime lords like himself. Trained by the KGB then left to their own devices to use their skills and global connections to amass great wealth once the Soviet Union was no more.

An alarm blared, followed by a gunshot, then two, then three, then several bursts of automatic weapons fire followed by screams of agony. Worst were the screams that came without preceding gunfire, that echoed from the silence. They had seen what Tyrell's knife had done to Tatiana's imbecile of a husband. Kazimir had brought Andreyev the photos of the room where Levi had been savagely disarticulated, an explosion of blood, meat, organs, and bone decorated every surface of that room, dripping from the walls and furniture as if a grenade had gone off inside the man. And Byrd assured him that Levi had been alive for most of the carnage, watching as his body was unmade piece by piece. Those images were fresh in Andreyev's mind as he listened to the screams of his men. He could only imagine what Tyrell was doing to them.

Andreyev nodded again. This was a nod of acceptance,

of a man at peace with his fate. Yet, his eyes betrayed fear. Getting a bullet in the skull, a quick death, was not something Andreyev feared. It would almost be a mercy compared to the slow, rotting, dehumanizing end promised to him by the cancer. But pain, the kind of pain this assassin delighted in, that was a cause for mortal terror.

Kazimir's phone rang. He answered it as he strode quickly toward the window to see what was going on outside.

"What the fuck is happening out there?" Kazimir barked into the phone as he parted the curtains and gazed out over the front yard. Fyodor, a young man who'd just recently come on board as a favor to his father who'd died more than a decade ago in service to Andreyev, lay face down on the front lawn in a pool of his own blood. Kazimir took a step back, away from the window, and reached for the gun in his holster. His face told Andreyev what he clearly already knew, what the continuing wails of anguish confirmed.

"He's here," Andreyev stated.

"Yes, sir."

Andreyev took another deep breath of oxygen, then let out a few wheezing, phlegm-choked coughs. He wondered how many breaths he had left before he went to meet his fallen comrades, his wife Illyana, and perhaps even his son Gregor, who'd died three days after being born.

"Call Mr. Byrd back. Tell him to come collect his pet monster."

"Yes, sir. I will call him."

"And, Kazimir, go home. You have served me well. I am dying anyway, but you have many years yet ahead of you. You don't have to die with me."

Andreyev could see the indecision overcome his bodyguard's features for a brief moment before they relaxed once again into their usual stoic resolve.

"I will stop this man. You will not die today."

"Okay, Kazimir. Okay," Andreyev replied. His voice did not sound convinced.

Kazimir went to the gun safe in the closet and pulled out an AK-47. He had his Glock 9mm still in the shoulder holster he wore over his shirt, but he presumed he would need more firepower for the monster outside making his men scream. He walked over to the bedroom door and locked it, then returned to Andreyev's side. He punched Byrd's number into his phone. The man answered on the first ring.

"Your killer is here," Kazimir said. "Come get him off my lawn."

He dropped the phone and hefted the AK, taking a shooters stance, waiting for Tyrell to show his face so he could put holes in it, but knowing it would not be that easy.

An abrupt silence crushed the air from the room. Both men knew what that signified. All their men were dead. There was no one left to kill but them.

The lights went out. Kazimir handed the Glock to his boss. He kept the AK aimed straight ahead into the darkness as he placed himself between Andreyev and the locked bedroom door.

"I will protect you, sir. I will protect you."

Andreyev wished his bodyguard's voice didn't tremble so much when he said those words. It would have been nice to be able to believe him.

The window exploded. Kazimir whirled around with the AK and fired out into the night through the shattered glass. Then the bedroom door blew open. Kazimir turned and

Fight For Me 195

ripped off a few rounds in that direction as well. Andreyev had not yet fired a shot.

"Show yourself! Come in here and get me! I am waiting for you!" Kazimir yelled into the darkness.

There was no reply.

The room was cloudy with gun smoke, which made the darkness even more opaque. No, it wasn't gun smoke, Kazimir realized. It was a smoke grenade. The only reason the assassin would have thrown a smoke grenade into the room was if he planned on sneaking in without being seen. Kazimir looked around the room. He couldn't see a thing. His ears were still ringing from the gunfire, so it was useless to listen for footsteps. It was the perfect cover for someone to tip toe into the room.

"Drop your gun, Kazimir. It's over, my friend," he heard Andreyev say from behind him. The big bodyguard turned and saw through the darkness and smoke, a woman with a gun pointed at his boss's head. She was crouched down low, using Andreyev as a shield. Kazimir thought he might be able to shoot her before she pulled the trigger. Maybe, if he'd been carrying a different gun, and he wasn't breathing so hard, and his heart wasn't trying to pound its way through his ribcage, he could shoot her without hitting the old man. But those were not the circumstances he found himself in. If he tried to shoot her now, he'd cut Andreyev in half. But, then, he might have a chance to survive himself.

Kazimir considered his many years of service to Andreyev. The man had been like a father to him. Rescuing him from an orphanage when he was fifteen years old, already past the age when any family would have wanted to adopt him, already stealing and fighting and selling drugs, trying to build a nest egg for the inevitable moment when he would be kicked out of the orphanage and would have to fend for himself. Andreyev had found him breaking into a car, Andreyev's car. Kazimir had just jimmied open the lock when strong hands grabbed him and yanked him off his feet, roughly tossing him to the ground. The old man stood above him with his bodyguard pointing a gun down at him. Andreyev had only been in his late forties at the time, still old to a fifteen-year-old kid. Kazimir had always thought of him as "the old man." The bodyguard, a tall, burly, gray-haired man with steel-colored eyes and lips so thin they appeared to be little more than a slash cut into his face, had been prepared to kill him. Kazimir stuck out his chin and looked the bodyguard in the eyes.

"Go ahead. Kill me. I don't care." He meant that then. He had nothing to live for. Dying would have been preferable to winding up a homeless vagrant someday. Andreyev gestured toward his bodyguard, waving him off with a flick of the wrist. The bodyguard put his gun away and stepped back as the old man stepped forward, eying Kazimir with curiosity and amusement.

"How old are you, boy?"

"Fifteen."

"And what is your name?"

"Kazimir Taktarov."

"Why are you breaking into cars instead of in school, Kazimir? Where are your parents?"

"I don't have any parents."

"They are dead?"

Kazimir shrugged. "I don't know. I never met them."

"You were abandoned?"

Kazimir nodded.

"I live in the orphanage"

Andreyev nodded.

"I understand," Adreyev said, opening his wallet and

Fight For Me

giving the boy a business card and a fifty dollar bill, American money. "Call me. I will give you a job and a place to live. If you work hard, you will never be hungry again, never have to go back to that orphanage"

Kazimir had worked hard. He'd grown into Andreyev's most loyal soldier. His most trusted. The old man's right hand. But he was no longer as callous about his own life as he'd been as a fifteen-year-old vagrant. He cared about it quite a bit now. He had a wife, a mistress, and seven children between the two of them. He'd just bought a house big enough for all of them and was planning to tell his wife about his other family and move them all in together. She would protest, but, ultimately, she would relent. She hadn't loved him in many years, but she respected him as the provider of the family, and his word was law. He imagined them all living happily together, but not if he was dead. He didn't want his kids growing up in an orphanage somewhere, like him.

"Sorry, sir." Kazimir raised the AK, aiming it at the woman and his boss. He never got off a shot.

26

I wasn't sure Master's plan would work, but I deferred to his expertise in the matter. Eviscerating the last three guards instead of shooting them quickly like we had the others seemed reckless. Master had insisted that terrorizing the old gangster and his men would make them sloppy, more likely to make mistakes. I knew it was more than that. Master was enjoying the carnage. He was intoxicated by the bloodshed. His eyes sparkled like a coke fiend as he stabbed, slit throats, and even carved out the eyes of the surprisingly few Russian mafioso guarding Mr. Krovopuskov's mansion. I counted just over half a dozen. Easy work, Master had assured me. Still, taking time to torture and mutilate the guards was an unnecessary risk.

I lost track of how many guards I shot. Three? Four? I was terrified. Couldn't seem to catch my breath. I felt like I was going to faint. Bullets whizzed by my head. One struck my vest and knocked the wind out of me. But Master and I were still alive, and there didn't seem to be much opposition left.

The last guard downstairs died horribly. At least, I hope

he was dead. Master stabbed the guard in the lower abdomen, then used both hands to slowly saw his way upward, cutting all the way up to the sternum. The man's intestines unspooled and spilled from his torso. He left the guard lying on the front porch, screaming and wailing while trying to hold in his guts. Then, we went back into the house.

The guard whose eyes Master had carved out had given up Andreyev Krovopuskov's location. He was still in his bedroom. Locked in with his bodyguard. Master handed me something that looked like a grenade launcher.

"Smoke grenades. Once I shut off the lights, fire one through that big window on the second floor. That's Krovopuskov's bedroom. Then get your ass upstairs as fast as you can. You secure the old man. I'll take out the bodyguard."

I wanted to give him a final kiss, just in case one of us didn't make it, but Master was already turning away from me. He ran into the house, then ran back out and scooped me up into his blood-drenched, gore-soaked arms and kissed me. That kiss sucked out my soul and set my entire body ablaze. I wished it would never end, that we could just run away together right then and there, take a flight to some Caribbean island and be making love on a beach by this time tomorrow. When the kiss ended, and everything swam back into vivid focus, I saw Master's eyes. They looked soft, caring, they glistened with moisture.

"I love you, Athena."

It was so unexpected, I didn't have time to respond before he turned away again, moving quickly through the house. I wanted to shout after him, tell him that I loved him too, that I adored him, worshiped him, but he was gone. He'd pulled up the mansion's plans before we got there, so he knew where the circuit breaker was. He was going to

Fight For Me 201

shut off the lights. I needed to get into position to do my part.

I jogged around to the front of the house and positioned myself under the window where Krovopuskov and his bodyguard were holed up. I saw a curtain part and pressed myself against the house so I couldn't be seen, or shot, more importantly. A minute went by, then another, then all the lights went out. I stepped back into the center of the circular driveway and aimed the grenade launcher at the window. Then I fired. The grenade sailed through the window, shattering it, and gunfire sprayed the driveway, tearing up the asphalt a few yards from where I stood. Whoever was firing was just shooting blindly. They didn't know where I was. Another explosion, Master blasting open the door to Krovopuskov's bedroom, presumably, followed by more automatic weapons fire. I sprinted into the house and up the stairs to join my Master.

Master was still outside Krovopuskov's bedroom, crouched down low. He gestured for me to get down. I did as he said, crouching low into a duck walk. He waved his hand again, indicating he wanted me even lower. I dropped down onto my belly and began a military crawl toward him. He did the same, crawling through the bedroom door. I followed. He gestured for me to go to the left, toward Krovopuskov. He was my target.

I made it to the aging gangster without encountering any opposition. It was so dark in there, had Master not packed the night vision goggles, I would have been as blind as our prey, our meal. I stood and put my gun to the old gangster's temple, then relieved him of his gun.

"Tell your bodyguard to drop his weapon," I whispered into the ear of the once fearsome Andreyev Krovopuskov, now a withered husk, a shadow of his former self. Master had shown me photos of the man. We had researched him on the internet, and the minimal photos available had been like watching a man deteriorate in stop motion. He went from handsome, young, KGB agent, to withered septuagenarian in the span of a few photographs. It was hard to believe that this man in the wheelchair, sucking oxygen through a hose, was the one who had sent those men to our house.

"Drop your gun, Kazimir. It's over, my friend," Mr. Krovopuskov said.

I couldn't see the bodyguard's expression, but something in his posture, the way he hesitated for several long seconds, then lifted his rifle back up to his shoulder, told me he was not going to comply. I waited for the bullets to rip through me, happy that I had at least gotten to spend one last evening with the man I loved, my Master, who was on the floor beneath the big bodyguard, aiming the two .44 caliber Smith and Wesson revolvers he always kept in his shoulder holsters up at the bodyguard. He pulled both triggers, and the sound was like the report of a canon. The bodyguard's legs collapsed under him, and he fell in a heap, kicking and convulsing on the floor in his death throes.

Master stood and put his pistols back in their holsters. He removed his night vision goggles and walked over to the old gangster. He knelt down in front of Andreyev, leaning over so his face was inches from the Russian's.

"You should not have sent those men to my home, Andreyev. Did Byrd give you my address?"

"You already know the answer to this," Andreyev replied. "Do not make me die a snitch."

Master smiled humorlessly.

"You're right. You're right. I do."

He grabbed the old man by the forehead, then pushed

his head back, exposing his neck. He leaned in and seized the old man's throat in his teeth, biting down hard, thrashing his head back and forth like a dog ripping meat from a bone. The old Russian screamed as Master tore out a fist-sized chunk of the man's throat.

Master stood, spitting out Andreyev's cricoid cartilage, larynx, and a large mouthful of trachea, wiping the blood from his lips with the back of his hand. Andreyev Krovo-puskov, once one of the most feared criminals on earth, the kingmaker who helped elect presidents, died gargling his own blood with tears weeping from his eyes.

27

"THIS WAS THE EASY PART," MASTER SAID. WE WERE WALKING out of Krovopuskov's mansion, heading to our car. "Byrd will be prepared. He has other killers."

"Like you?" I asked.

Master shook his head.

"Not like me. They work for him. Byrd works for me. I got him into this business. He was just a computer geek working for an insurance company, upgrading their software, when I found him. I had him hack into the system at the company he worked for to make sure the widow of one of my meals got her payout."

"Why wouldn't she? Why weren't they going to pay her?"

"Because there was no body. Byrd fixed it, I paid him. Then I started using him for other things. A few years later, he was booking all my jobs for me and handling all the logistics. He's really good at what he does. Keeps up to date on all the latest software and technology, all the gossip on the dark web. Rarely makes mistakes. But he has gotten too big for his britches now that he has taken on other contractors. He has forgotten who's boss. I knew this day would come."

"Do you know where he is?"

"I know how to find him. We just need to find a place to rest while I make inquiries."

We had just reached the car when a volley of gunshots punched into Master's chest, dropping him to the ground.

"Master!"

There was blood, lots of blood. Whatever he had been shot with had gone straight through his vest. I raised my weapon and aimed at the three figures quickly approaching. I shot the first one in his big fat, grinning face. It exploded like a pumpkin, then I heard a couple shots ring out beside me. Master was still alive, and still deadly. He shot the other two, then climbed slowly back to his feet. He stood swaying, blood pouring from his injuries. I tried to help, but he pushed me away.

"Damnit, you're hurt! Let me help you!" I yelled, forgetting to add "Sir" or "Master." I would apologize for that later, if there was a later.

I draped Master's arm over my shoulder and wrapped an arm around his waist. One of the guys Master had shot was breathing rapidly, a rattling, whistling sound coming from the hole in his chest. The other one was still moving, struggling to get back to his feet. Master shot him in the leg, and the man fell over onto his back.

"Ow! Fuck! Stop! Fucking, stop!"

With my help, Master made it over to where the three men lay on the ground. He put two bullets in the skull of the one who was wheezing and choking, silencing him. The guy Master shot in the leg, a short man with a flabby belly that was incongruous with his thin arms and legs and long slender neck, rolled on the ground, holding his stomach.

Fight For Me   207

Blood spurted out between his fingers. Master kicked the man's gun away.

"Oh, God! Oh, God! I'm dying! I'm fucking dying!"

"Hello, Byrd. What are you doing here?" Master said, looking down at the man writhing on the floor beneath him.

"Help me, Tyrell. I'm sorry. I fucked up. I'll do whatever you want. I can fix all this!"

"You came out in the field to kill me? You actually got your soft, flabby ass out from behind your computer because that old, sick Russian told you to? You didn't learn anything I taught you. You disappoint me, Byrd. Goodbye"

"No! No! Don't!"

BLAM!!!

"Master? Master?"

Master collapsed. He lay on the driveway, beside Byrd's bleeding corpse. He had lost a lot of blood.

"You need to get out of here," Master said, pushing me away.

Sirens blared in the distance. Police were coming.

"I'm not leaving you."

"I'm dying, Athena. I'm not going to make it."

"No. No. We can get you fixed up. I'll take you to a hospital."

Master shook his head. He coughed up blood, choking on it for a moment before spitting out a large chunk of bloody phlegm.

I tried to lift him, but Master pulled me into his arms, hugging me against him.

"I love you, Athena."

"Master, no. You can't die. You can't leave me."

"You have to leave me."

I shook my head, tears flooded my eyes, and I began to sob. Big, ugly, sobs.

"I'm not leaving you, Sir!"

"You will do what I tell you. I am still your Master. Now, get the fuck out of here!"

He pushed me away again.

"Go!"

"I love you, Master."

"I love you too, Athena. You are released from my service," he said right before losing consciousness.

EPILOGUE

THE PRETTY BOY BOXER HURRIED OUT OF THE GYM, CRADLING his shattered arm. He had called me every gender-specific insult you could aim at a woman. Some of them I wasn't sure had been in use since the nineteenth century. A part of me considered finishing him off right there in the same cage David had died in a year ago. It was odd that it had already been a year. It still felt like yesterday when I had put out that first ad, when I found my Master and my life changed forever.

A part of me half expected him to come walking back through that door, back into the cage, to win me all over again. A sob caught in my throat. I knew I would never see him again. I remembered leaving him, hurt, bleeding on that Russian asshole's driveway. I should have saved him. I shouldn't have left him, no matter what he said. That was one time I should not have been his obedient slave. My mind kept going back and forth between being proud of myself for obeying him, for answering the question of whether my submission was contingent on his dominance, and being ashamed of myself for not going down with him, dying at his side if need be. My fear was that I would never again find anyone strong enough to be my Master.

This was the third such tournament I'd thrown in as many months. Instead of fighting each other, I now made the men seeking to win my submission fight me. Tyrell had made me a vicious, efficient killer and a ferocious fighter. I had yet to find my match.

"Okay. Who's next?" I asked, looking around the gym. There had been six when we started. I had already beaten two. Two more had left after I broke the boxer's arm. That should have left two more fighters, yet there were three. One of them, no more than a hundred and fifty pounds, wearing a hoodie with the hood up, obscuring their face, stood and walked toward the cage.

"Who are you?" I asked.

The fighter pulled the hoodie over their head, revealing a short buzz cut dyed black and pink, muscular shoulders and arms, and large, perky breasts.

"Don't tell me you forgot your best friend?"

My mouth fell open.

"Becca? What are you doing here?"

"I'm here for the tournament. Winner gets you as their slave, right? I'm here to fight for you."

I shook my head.

"Becca, I'm not the same person I was, not the same fighter. You'll get hurt."

Becca shook her head and scowled.

"Are you trying to offend me? I started training again, MMA. I even took a couple fights. Just because I'm not some big steroid freak like these assholes doesn't mean I can't still kick your ass."

"Okay, then. Let's fight."

"Two Dommes enter, one slave leaves."

Fight For Me

I laughed. That was actually pretty good. Maybe I'd put it in my next ad if no one won today.

The bell rang to start the round, and Becca threw a spinning back kick that caught me in the ribcage and nearly doubled me over, followed by a jumping snap kick that caught me under the chin and whipped my head back. I staggered, my legs felt like rubber. The room tilted and spun, but I was able to stay on my feet. I shook my head to clear the fog just as Becca charged in swinging a wild overhand right.

Hmmm? Maybe I had underestimated her after all.

I knew it was unlikely any man would ever live up to my Master. He had been like a god among men. Maybe no man ever would, but perhaps a woman? I wondered if Becca would prefer I call her Master or Mistress?

#End#

WRATH JAMES WHITE is a former World Class Heavyweight Kickboxer, a professional Kickboxing and Mixed Martial Arts trainer, distance runner, performance artist, and former street brawler, who is now known for creating some of the most disturbing works of fiction in print.

Wrath is the author of such extreme horror classics as THE RESURRECTIONIST (now a major motion picture titled "Come Back To Me") SUCCULENT PREY, and it's sequel PREY DRIVE, YACCUB'S CURSE, 400 DAYS OF OPPRESSION, SACRIFICE, VORACIOUS, TO THE DEATH, THE

REAPER, SKINZZ, EVERYONE DIES FAMOUS IN A SMALL TOWN, THE BOOK OF A THOUSAND SINS, HIS PAIN, POPULATION ZERO and many others. He is the co-author of TERATOLOGIST co-written with the king of extreme horror, Edward Lee, SOMETHING TERRIBLE co-written with his son Sultan Z. White, ORGY OF SOULS co-written with Maurice Broaddus, HERO and THE KILLINGS both co-written with J.F. Gonzalez, POISONING EROS co-written with Monica J. O'Rourke, and BOY'S NIGHT co-written with Matt Shaw among others.

Wrath lives and works in Austin, TX.